WHITE
TIME

Also by Margo Lanagan

Black Juice

WHITE
TIME

Margo Lanagan

An Imprint of HarperCollins*Publishers*

SC
L243W

ACKNOWLEDGMENTS

These stories were all written in the lead-up to, during, or immediately
after Clarion West Writers Workshop 1999. The instructors were Nancy
Kress, Octavia E. Butler, Greg Bear, Howard Waldrop, Gordon van
Gelder, and Gwyneth Jones, and I thank them for their inspiring and
generous tuition.

Big thanks also to my fellow workshoppers, whose large- and
small-scale help is evident on every one of these pages. Sarah Brandel,
Christine Castigliano, Duncan Clark, Sandy Clark, Monte Cook, Dan
Dick, Andrea Hairston, Jay Joslin, Leah Kaufman, Ama Patterson, Liz
Roberts, Joe Sutliff Sanders, Tom Sweeney, Sheree Renée Thomas,
Trent Walters, and Steve Woodworth—that was a great six weeks.

And thanks to Dave Myers, Leslie Howle, and the Clarion West
alumni for all their work and support.

Last but definitely not least, thanks to my family—Steven, Jack, and
Harry—for letting me go.

Library of Congress Cataloging-in-Publication Data
Lanagan, Margo.
    White time / Margo Lanagan.— 1st American ed.
        p.   cm.
    Summary: Presents ten short stories, both dark and hopeful, that journey into the
past, the future, and altered versions of the present.
    ISBN-10: 0-06-074393-X (trade bdg.) — ISBN-13: 978-0-06-074393-2 (trade bdg.)
    ISBN-10: 0-06-074394-8 (lib. bdg.) — ISBN-13: 978-0-06-074394-9 (lib. bdg.)
    1. Children's stories. [1. Interpersonal relations—Fiction. 2. Conduct of life—
Fiction. 3. Short stories.] I. Title.
PZ7.L216Whi 2006   2005019755
[Fic]—dc22   CIP
                                                                             AC

Typography by R. Hult
1 2 3 4 5 6 7 8 9 10
❖
First American Edition
First published in Australia by Allen & Unwin Publishers, 2000

11/2006

WHITE

TIME

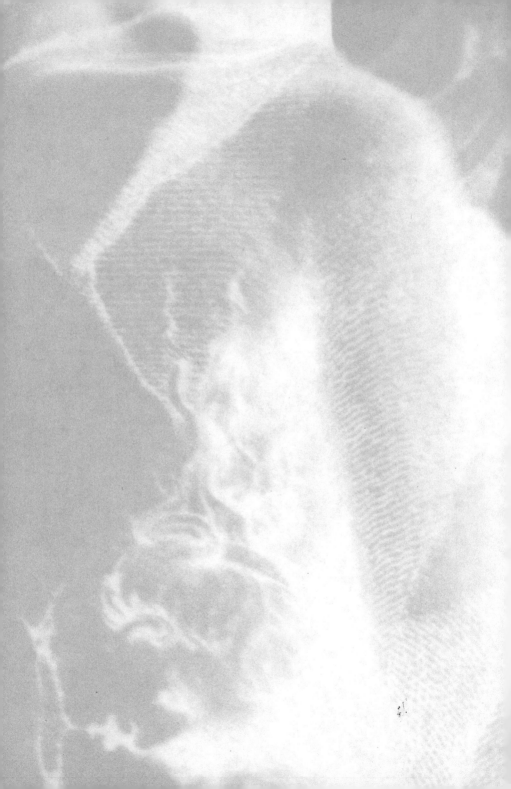

Student: Sheneel Carpenter
Occupation: General process walk-through
Workplace: Commonweal White Time
              Laboratories
Date: Spring semester break

"Buggaration." Sheneel crumpled the hard copy, tossed it bin-wards and banged her head a few times on the desk.

"What's up?" said Dalma, taking a break from her victory dance with Keanu.

"It's not fair! You two *always* get what you want. You both get to go on release-party tasting, and I end up at the bloody White Time Labs!"

"White time? What'd you put that down for, dope?"

"You had to put down a second choice."

"You just shouldn't've! Keanu's brother said, don't you remember? You don't give 'em any *choice* but what you want!" She danced off again.

"White time'll be *interesting* . . . won't it?" said Liv Morrow. She hadn't even opened her letter. She already knew she'd be tasting her dad's fashionorium, making antique musical instruments, which she did in her spare time anyway, but being paid for it and doing it to fixed hours.

"It'll be boring as hell," moaned Sheneel. "*They* get to choose dance music and do celebrity bites and put out gazines. We were all going to do it *together*—that was the *whole idea*."

"Yeah," said Liv, "but tasting's supposed to be about

the sort of job you want to have after school. I mean, you want to end up some terrible *ageing groover?*"

"Come on, Liv—I'm only in Year 10!"

"And release parties are pretty seasonal—like, six weeks at the end of every school year. And you have to be right there, like, in *front* of the cutting edge to make any kind of a living."

"They're pretty *fun*, that's all I know." Sheneel pretended to weep.

Liv smiled and patted her on the shoulder. "Never mind. White time could be fun, too."

"Yeah, right. Fun like menstru-*ation* is fun. Fun like tidying your *room* is fun."

Liv laughed. Leaning confidentially against her, she said in a soft, super-reasonable Sir-voice, "Well, both of those things can 'be their own reward'—"

"No," said Sheneel severely. "Don't start."

Sir was doing a tour of the classroom. "And you, Keanu?"

"Release party, too, Sir."

"*Another* release party? They're taking a lot this year, aren't they?"

"Not enough," said Sheneel.

Joey Fitzardo sniggered. "Yeah, poor old Sheneel copped the Commonweal Labs. Hoot!"

"Really?" Sir brightened. "Thinking about a career in time theory, Sheneel?"

"No, *Sir!*"

"Pushing the envelope in ethical hazards, maybe?"

"Oh, don't be cruel, Sir."

"Never mind, Sheneel. I'm sure you'll find something there to interest you."

"I think it's going to majorly *suck*, Sir," said Sheneel,

and was gratified at the general laugh she got.

Sir's eyes went bland again. "Well, I look forward to reading your report."

| | | |

Taster's general remarks:
This was a very interesting assignment. I got to see all the interesting things White Time do in the white time reservoirs, met lots of interesting people and learned a lot.

| | | |

"A what?" said the guy at the terminal.

"An occupation-taster," said the reception-guy patiently.

"Like I said, a what?" He hadn't stopped keyboarding since the reception-guy had brought Sheneel in.

"All you have to do is take her with you, Lon, and show her what you do, what it entails. Your job."

"Ah. What we used to call work experience," the guy brayed, "back in the old days before the work/leisure dichotomy became politically incorrect." What was he *talking* about?

"And try not to turn her into an old cynic like you." The reception-guy winked at Sheneel and abandoned her there.

The place was a mess. Everything was grey—not dirty, but made of grey plastic. Cables and plugs and dead computers and bits of nameless equipment. *Stuff*, piled on the grey tables and in all the grey corners. Nowhere for anyone to sit, except him. Mr. Keyboarding. Mr. Whistling-to-Himself. Lon.

"'ka-ay," he said finally, eyes still on the screen. "Looks like we've got one or two for you this morning. For your viewing enner-tainment."

A few random white spots showed on the screen, on a grey ground between two elaborate toolbars. Lon blanked the screen without explaining anything. "C'mon, then."

The elevator took them *way* down. There was nothing to show how far, just an intercom in the metal wall.

"I better give you the tourist spiel, I guess," said Lon. Not once had he met eyes with her.

"I didn't know tourists were allowed in here."

"They're not. Curious bureaucrats, I mean; historians; people who've got business here, or think they might have." He inspected the top four corners of the elevator ceiling. "Okay. What I am, is a field officer. Meaningless name. I used to be called a redirection agent, but someone decided that was too straightforward."

This guy is a sour old bucket, thought Sheneel. *This is going to be fun, I don't think.*

"You know what white time is?" He sounded dead bored.

"Sort of . . . We did it in school, a bit . . ."

"Time out of time, people call it, but they're wrong. It's all time, like white light is all colours, or white noise is all pitches of noise coming at you together. White time's all over the place, blobs and puddles of it, some just hanging in space, some buried in planets, like ours here. This one's quite a big reservoir. Took a bit of clearing—I wasn't here, back when they first happened on it. It keeps one field officer—*moi*—occupied full-time; plenty of eggheads clack-ulating behind the scenes, too. All very interesting, if you like number and time theories. Do you?" He shot Sheneel a look so sharp she flinched.

"Um . . . *number*'s okay, I suppose."

"Huh. Gal after my own heart. I can't stand time-theorists. Bane of my existence, them and their 'spiritual dimension.' Bloody god-botherers. Anyway! What I do. I redirect . . . entities, we call 'em. They're actually bodies. Physical beings." He frowned and fell quiet.

Sheneel thought he might be trying to protect her delicate sensibilities. "D'you mean corpses?"

He looked startled. "Bloody hell, no." He really had quite okay eyes. He'd probably been good-looking once. "What gave you that idea?"

Sheneel shrugged again. "You said *bodies* . . ."

"Yeah, as in, *not*-bits-of-white-time, is all I meant. No, they're alive, all right. Just kind of stuck. Between heart-beats, if you know what I mean."

She didn't. "How far down are we going?"

"Coupla k's. Don't fret, it'll be a while yet. Okay, so what we'll be doing is, we'll suit you up, put some pips in your ears. Then we'll head out and score us an entity or two. I have to warn you, it's gravity-free in there. You got any problems with that? No? Guess it's pretty ordinaire these days for you kids, with your arcades. Used to be hot stuff in my time. Tourists got a bit of a thrill, swimming out into 'space' there."

Sheneel smiled wanly. Dalma was probably talking to Dylan Lazzaro right this minute, giggling and getting him to autograph her cling-shirt.

| | | |

How is a typical day structured?

Lon Klegg usually spends the morning redirecting entities in white time. He eats lunch in the very well-stocked canteen, talks to colleagues about what he found that morning, and in the afternoon does equipment maintenance.

| | | |

The elevator's tone changed and Lon stood away from the wall. The cube shuddered and stopped, and the doors opened on another grey room, slightly less piled with equipment.

"Let's see if I can find a suit that fits you."

The suit he chose had been profusely sweated in by the previous wearer. "This *stinks*!" said Sheneel, glad she'd worn jeans and the long-sleeved drill shirt.

"Well, you can stink or you can flop around in a size one-oh-two."

She eyed the monstrous 102 and kept pulling on the smelly suit.

Lon spent a long time finding pips her size and swapping batteries around. "Finally," he said. He fitted the left-hand pip into her ear; it was playing quiet, wandering music. He plugged in the right-hand one, and the other half of her head filled with the sound of Lon's breathing, then his metallicised voice: "Howzat?"

"Coming through loud and clear."

He snatched his own right-ear pip out. "Crikey mama, don't shout, girl. What's your name again? Sharelle?"

"Sheneel."

"Oh, yeah. Remember that. When you talk to me in

there, use my name: Lon. When I talk to you, I'll use yours. And if I get it wrong, tell me, okay? Or you might turn into a Sharelle."

She laughed politely.

"I mean it."

He put the suit's soft helmet on her, and strapped a squashy bag onto her back. "Reserve oxygen," he said. "I've never had to use it, so don't get toey."

"How long are we going to be in there?"

"No time at all, mate. Why?"

"Does it matter that I'm starting to need to go to the toilet?"

He shook his head inside his suit-helmet. "It won't get any worse while you're in there."

He led her into the transition chamber, a grey tube in the wall full of tech-head stuff, glass-sealed at both ends. It was a little small for both of them, and he was fiddling with the front of her suit, attaching tubes, growling to himself. She tried to think of some technical-type question to hide her embarrassment.

"So, when you say 'redirecting,' where are you redirecting the things *to*?"

He looked disconcerted. "Well. How do I put it? These guys we pick up, they think they want to get to a particular point in time, right? Don't ask me why—it's just a phase everything goes through on its way up the evolutionary ladder, eh. Is time travel still *cool*, or has it gotten passé, too?"

"Well, there's lots of games about it, I guess, lots of movies . . ."

"Anyway, before they work out how to do it properly, they go through the stage of flinging themselves out of their own time and expecting to go to whenever they want, but to stay in exactly the same spot in the meta-universe as they started from. And, well, they do, but the trouble is, their planet or dust cloud or interstitial residence has moved on, see? What with your planets and galaxies orbiting, and your less predictable universal shifts. You following me?"

"So why don't they just die? Like, if they end up in the middle of a comet, or in dead space or something?"

"Well, possibly they do. 'Evidence has yet to be found,' as they say. But some of them, for some reason, end up in white time, in places like this." Lon poked a thumb at the other door. "The current theory is that the time travel process actually *makes* these reservoirs happen."

Sheneel felt her brain struggling. "So do they go to, like, the bit of white time that's closest to their usual place in the . . . the meta-universe?"

"Another good question. You'd have to ask the number-crunchers upstairs that one. They're the ones looking at the 'big picture.' I only work on the local council. I only risk my life on a daily basis. Just kidding." And he flashed her a pretend smile.

| | | |

The chamber door swung outward into darkness. *Stupid question number umpteen*, thought Sheneel. *What made me think white time would be white?*

"Push out as far as you can, first off," said Lon. "Don't worry, you won't hit anything. There's nothing to hit." He shot away.

"I thought we were underground!" she called after him.

His right hand clapped to his head. "Shout like that

once more, Sheneel, and you're up top with the number-crunchers for the day."

"Sorry." She pushed off hard into the nothingness. It didn't feel as if she was moving unless she watched the door-circle recede behind her, its light playing on the out-feed coils.

"'kay." There was a clunk in her voice-pip. Lon twirled as he reached the end of his push. The light set into the suit of his chest lit up several—well, "entities" was the only name Sheneel had for them—suspended like soft drink spilled in an anti-gravity café. They looked as if they'd suddenly lit up from within, because there was nothing in the darkness between them and Lon's chest to create a beam of light.

"Now, Shanelle, I've got to—"

"Sheneel."

"Sheneel, I've got to stabilise us. It's up to Rowan in the tap room to move us about, so you'll hear him and me swapping coordinates a bit. Say hello to the young lady, Rowan."

"Hi, Sheneel." A younger, brighter voice than Lon's was in her head.

"We'll do the biggest first, Ro. She's a monster, mate."

They floated past two pale, person-sized sacs that pulsed like jellyfish in the darkness. Sheneel looked around for the bigger entity, but there seemed to be nothing more between them and the distant blotched surface of the wall . . . hang on, did white time *have* a wall?

Then she was scrabbling and pedalling on the end of her cable. "*That's* an entity? That bloody great—How big is it?"

"Whoa, whoa," said Rowan. "You're not in danger, Sheneel."

"What *is* it?"

"Mind my ears, girl," grumbled Lon.

She squashed her voice down. "Lon! Is it *alive?*" She was still trying to fight Rowan's steering her towards the thing.

"Well, as I said, it's not alive and it's not dead, Sheneel. Cool it, girl. It'll be gone in a sec. Hang in there and watch."

Rowan stopped moving her, and she hung still, panting. Lon floated on, a shadow against the gradually shrinking circle his chest-light threw. Then he hung still, a small knot of light and shadow applying himself to the entity's surface. There were growths and stains all over it, encrustations bigger than Lon.

"Okay, give it to me, Rowan," he said. "This bit's just maths, Sheneel. Just punching numbers into a clackulator."

"You've already made that calculator joke today, Sir— Lon, I mean!" It had nearly happened to her. She had nearly forgotten his name. "Am I supposed to tell you stuff like that?"

"It can only help, girl."

She waited. Her head was so *busy*, with the two voices blabbing numbers in one ear, and the music wandering in the other. It was annoying. She wanted to unplug everything and just hear for herself what white time sounded like. She was sure it would be a delicious, restful silence. She put her gloved hand to her helmet, and the two surfaces ran slickly off each other. The pips had been tiny, and had gone deep into her ears; she was stuck with the breathing and the blabbing and the tuneless tinkling.

And then the wall—the entity—was not there. It vanished without sound or vibration. Only the afterimage of

Lon's chest-light on the blotched skin burned out against an entity-free blackness.

"That was it? Lon?"

"Sheneel. That's what we do."

"What was it?"

"Thing called a Whalan. If you think of the universe as an ocean, that thing is a deep-sea bottom-crawler. A big prawn, that's all. A space-cockroach."

"You've seen one before?"

"I've heard of 'em. What's your name again?"

"Sheneel. And you're Lon."

"Let's go back and get those two little fellas."

The two jellyfish had become very like people, Sheneel thought. But a moment later they were like branching vein-networks, and then they were like branches, and then branches with leaves, and then like branch-less leaves clumped on the air. "Oh, *these* guys," said Lon. "We get quite a few of them through here, Sheneel. They're big history buffs."

"How come they keep changing?"

"They're similising. Playing off our brains. Trying to identify themselves to us, showing us a few things we know, things they might be like. It's automatic; it's not like they're communicating with us or anything warm and fuzzy like that. I'll put a sucker on each one, Rowan; my guess is, these two are travelling together." He attached two tiny suction cups to a leaf of each being, and keyed in numbers on a floating pad cabled to his belt. As he keyed, the two beings became stretched-out birds, rather ugly, without wings. "Am I right, Romo?"

"My name's Sheneel."

"He means me, Sheneel—Rowan." The birds vanished. "And yes, Lon, they were together."

"Geez," said Sheneel. "When's this music in my ear going to *do* something? When's a hummable bit going to happen?"

"Never," said Rowan. "That's the point—nothing repetitive. Your brain needs it to keep time going inside your suit."

| | | |

What is the aspect of the tasting that you
enjoyed the least?
    The way white time scrambles your brain.

| | | |

In the suit-room, Lon drew the voice-pip out of her ear by its cord. She felt the weirdest alarm—would he stop breathing if she didn't listen? She had to restrain herself from snatching the pip back.

"Oh," she said, and pulled out the music-pip herself. "It's *really* quiet now."

She followed Lon's example and unzipped her cumbersome suit. It didn't seem to smell so bad now. And it had been well ventilated. Why had the guy before her— the "tourist" before her—got in such a sweat-bath?

In the elevator Lon sighed enormously and seemed to wake up a little. "You doing a walk-through, are you? Well, you've seen the best bit. The rest's pretty technical: testing equipment, filling out bloody stats sheets."

"You do this every morning?"

"Every couple of days." He watched her politely suppress a grimace. "Why, what do you think?"

She *tried* to think, and shrugged. "It's pretty strange . . ."

He was looking at her as if he expected her to say something more. Something clever, maybe. Something *insightful*, to use one of Sir's favourite words. She felt a flash of resentment; she wouldn't've *had* to be insightful on release-party tasting.

She smiled lamely and didn't say anything. And he didn't say anything back. And they rumbled on upwards, and at last came out into the labs, where she could sense other people—suddenly she could hardly wait to see other people.

Lon seemed to feel the same. "Toilets are down that way, canteen's up the other end. I'll meet you there, eh."

The canteen was thinly sprinkled with technicians, casually dressed. Something smelled yummy—lasagne. The server moved like a snail, pausing to chat with his colleagues, taking so long Sheneel felt like stomping in behind the bain-marie and serving her-bloody-self. *Finally* she had the food on her tray, and she was all shaky with hunger—she wanted to put her face down and take a big mouthful then and there.

Lon saw her making ready to sit a couple of tables away from his group. "Here, Sheneel." Grr. She'd really rather have a rest from him and his weird job, thanks. But she wasn't rude enough for that; over she went and took the seat next to him.

Everyone else had little snack-plates with half a cake or a bit of salad on them—except Lon, whose meal-plate was scraped so clean of lasagne you'd've thought it just came out of a dishwasher.

Sheneel didn't want to talk, just eat. "I'm so hungry," she apologised through her first mouthful.

"Yeah, it does that," said Lon.

The others were talking incomprehensibly. Lon

listened intently, unbuttoning his check shirt-sleeve. He pulled it up to his elbow and peeled off a patch there, pressed it under a broken foil in a cycle-packet on the table, broke out a fresh patch and took some care choosing a place on his inner forearm to stick it. Sheneel stopped chewing and stared at the circular imprints of previous patches, some livid, some just brownish shadows. Far out. A patch man—a "person with a physiological dependency," that is.

The shirt-sleeve swooshed down like a closing curtain. Lon was watching her. "Go on, ask," he said softly. Everyone else was still talking.

She pointed to her full mouth, chewed as long as she could hoping he'd be distracted by something. He wasn't. But she wouldn't ask the obvious question, the one he wanted to answer—she wouldn't give him the satisfaction.

"You take that right out here in the open?" she said, nodding around at the public-ness of the canteen, the bright, unsecretive light.

He slid the cycle-pack into his shirt pocket. "It's allowed," he said. "I'm allowed it. Special dispensation," he added slowly, as if to a child—a really little kid, not someone nearly finished school, like Sheneel. He tapped the side of his nose stagily. She was filled with equal parts dislike and uncertainty.

Lon stopped mugging. "It's so I can do the work. Anyone who does this for a while needs to go on patches. You've seen it: white time puts the screws on your brain."

Then one of the technicians said, "Anyway, we're not going to solve this today. Who've we got here, Lon? Someone who's been swimming in puddles, by the look of it."

Sheneel tried to smile politely and take a fairly big mouthful at the same time.

"This is Sheneel. She's on a walk-through. Don't worry, you'll get a chance to drivel in her ear this arvo—don't have to do it now and bore the pants off us."

"Hi, Sheneel. I'm Fare McCutcheon. I'm in Analysis."

Sheneel reluctantly put her fork down and shook hands. Fare was partly being polite, partly showing off.

"And this is Rowan, whose dulcet tones you would have heard already."

A guy who looked way too young to be working here gave her a shy smile. He had a nice face, but his haircut, or lack of, and that greenish knit vest, marked him as a hopeless style-munster. "Hi, Sharelle-Shanelle-Sheneel," he said.

"Hi, Romo."

"Okay, okay," said Lon. "That's enough, you two."

"How was it, Sheneel?" said Rowan.

"It was fine. Weird, but fine."

"Mind-broadening?"

Lon snorted.

"Mind-crumpling, more like," she said.

"You wait till Fare gets a-hold of you," said Lon. "This morning'll look like a piece a cake."

Fare grinned at him, a grin full of in-jokes and layers of meaning. "Ah, Lon, admit it. We need each other."

"Well, *you* need *me*."

Fare looked stung, gathered himself to strike back, then stopped and cast Sheneel a glance. He checked Lon's face and relaxed. "You. You're just a big tease, Lon Klegg."

Sheneel looked up at Lon. There was a ghost of

something there, maybe, in the creases around his eyes. *Oh, so he <u>could</u> smile properly, if he wanted to.*

| | | |

What aspect of the tasting did you enjoy
the most?
   The food in the canteen, especially on
field mornings!

| | | |

When Dalma saw Sheneel in the parkway, she flung out her arms. "I'm niched! I'm well and truly niched!"

"Lucky you," said Sheneel coldly.

"So how was the lab?" Dalma dropped her mini-pack on the grass and sat down.

"You don't wanna know. You're just being polite. You can't wait to show me where Lazzaro signed your shirt."

Dalma edged her jacket slowly off her shoulder, growling some strip-club music.

"Oh, bugga," said Sheneel. "He did it. You got it."

"He did it!" Dalma exposed a scramble of tag-letters across her shoulder blade. "It tickled like anything, but I got it." The top half of her body did a little dance. "Where's Joey? He was gunna meet me here—oh, there! Joey! Honestly, we've been having the bestest-best time, 'Neel. Haven't we, Jo?"

"What a place, eh? They work you to the bone! I'm dead!" Joey fell over flat on the grass.

"Oh, it's gunna be one great party, Sheneel. Guess who's going to be the opener!"

Sheneel played the game for a while, guessed and

exclaimed and watched Dalma fizz. Keanu joined them, too, and a couple of other release-party tasters, and Liv Morrow.

"But you weren't even there, Sheneel," Liv said suddenly, after a burst of laughter. "Where were you again?"

"Ooh, she was in white ti-ime," said Joey. "Floating around with the universal spookies!"

Liv laughed with the others. "So how was that?"

Everyone was listening. Sheneel looked around and realised how unusual this was, the group's faces all being turned to her. And she saw quite clearly that Dalma, Joey, and Keanu didn't expect much from her, were just looking to milk whatever she said for laughs.

She tried for world-weariness. "Thanks a lot, Liv— actually, I was trying to *forget* where I'd been." Which was true enough. And it worked for getting the eyes off her: Dalma squeaked, "Well, *we* don't want to *ever* forget where we were today, do we?" and there followed much cheering and high-fiving.

But, "Why?" said Liv, under cover of all that. "Was it scary, or just boring?"

Sheneel drew her knees up to her chest. She could smell the sweaty white-time suit in the cloth of her shirt, in the knees of her jeans. She tried for an answer but could only shake her head.

"Or neither?" joked Liv. "Hey, choose your own description."

Sheneel kept trying. "I just don't understand," she said eventually, "how people can go back to some jobs, day after day, year after year . . ."

Liv gave her a funny look, smiling but with a raised eyebrow. "What, you don't understand the jobbishness of jobs?"

"Mmph . . ." No, that wasn't what she meant. If a job drove you to *patches*—

"You don't get why all jobs can't be *fun?*"

Sheneel shot her a look. "Now you're laughing at me."

"Yeah," Liv apologised. "But I'll tell you—people go back to their jobs day after day because they have to."

"Have to? Well, there's having to and *having* to, isn't there? I mean—"

"They need the dough and they're doing something they can do. Don't you think?"

But that flying thought was gone. Liv's needling had thrown her off; Sheneel didn't know *what* she'd meant to say. "I suppose," she said miserably, just to shut Liv up.

| | | |

She had a day and a half with the number-crunchers, the brains on sticks. It was deadly dull. They kept *telling* her how interesting it was, but their jobs all seemed to be about feeding numbers into computers and getting different numbers out, and they never could quite tell her the point of it all. They tried, but they'd spent so long in these jobs that they talked in a kind of code, and couldn't seem to remember how to translate back to normal speech. She could feel Fare's intensity when he told her they were doing "nothing less than building a composite picture of the face of God," but the words were a meaningless combination; the purpose was still a mystery to her.

The third morning she was rostered in with Lon again.

He'd had the size 95 suit cleaned. "Hey, thanks!" she

said, surprised. He gave her a sober wink.

It was restful for her brain, just to float about and check out the entities.

"What's the weirdest one of these you've ever found, Lon?" she asked, her own voice metallic in her ear.

His breathing became thoughtful, and went on so long she thought his mind must have drifted off her question.

"Lon?"

"Sheneel. Just thinking."

"That little guy last summer was pretty weird." Rowan's tinned voice barged into her brain.

"Ah, yeah," said Lon. "Hard to get a fix on. Had to kind of scoop it up in the intake sucker, and then put the other one on him separately. He wasn't weird though, Ro. Just little."

"He was weird when you went down the trail and looked at where he came from."

"Yeah, well, I don't get to see all that. The weirdest, actually . . . Sheneel . . . are the ones most people'd think were the boringest. The humanish ones. That look like they could just wake up and walk out of here and start living along with us. But you know they couldn't. You know they'd go nuts, or explode, or die of some scratch or some food. The different-ness of things that seem alike—that's the wonder of the universe. Get us over to that CB–5 next, okay, Rowan?"

"You're on, Lon."

Lon shone his chest-light on the dolphin-sized, tentacled vertebrate as they approached. This wasn't the first one Sheneel had seen him deal with.

"At school they always say it's the opposite way round . . ." she said, then fell silent, confused by her brain having sprouted such a thought.

"They do?" Lon breathed in her head.

"Yeah, they're always going on about patterns and similarities and the intertext of all things, and how basically you and I are . . . are CB–5s, too."

"Oh yeah, *basically*. Basically we're all gas and water, aren't we? That's *helpful*." He reached out and touched the belt of her suit as Rowan positioned her at ninety degrees to him beside the CB–5. Her chest-light snapped on and Lon used it in conjunction with his own to choose two points along the creature's spine to place his suction cups. The CB–5 flinched a little as he placed them: "He'll have a dream," said Lon. He keyed in his "clack-ulations," the CB–5 vanished and the cups again floated at the ends of their leads.

Lon looked at her in puzzlement.

"I'm Sheneel," she said, before he had a chance to ask. She was getting used to the timing of his brain-scrambles. "Here for work experience. Your name's Lon."

"Ah, yes. Patterns. Sheneel. There's a reason why you look different from me. There's a reason why the stripes are different on every zebra."

Rowan chuckled in her head. "And you sneer when Fare goes on about spiritual dimensions, Lon. I can't believe I'm hearing this."

"Believe what you like, button-pusher," Lon muttered.

"I heard that."

"You were meant to. Get us over to that sea cow."

"That Third-phase Non-porous Intertemporal Vehicle, you mean?"

"Ah, shaddap."

| | | |

"So how's Miss Commonweal?" Dalma looked out from the release-party group picnicking under "their" tree in the park.

Sheneel laughed and drew a halo in the air above her own head. "Actually, I'm quite getting to like it."

"Ew, is she now?"

"*Actually*, I think you're off your rocker."

"Warning, warning—transformation to nigel-mode beginning."

The whole group squirmed at its own wit.

"Are you *serious*?" said Dalma disgustedly.

"Well, I have to admit, it's kind of interesting," Sheneel apologised. "Seeing all the different aliens and so on."

"'And so on'!" said Keanu. "Like, what else is there? Prayer meetings? Proofreading number sheets? Woo-woo!"

"Is Liv around?" Sheneel asked the boy at her feet.

But he was too new. "Liv? Who's Liv?" She could see he wasn't sure how much scorn to put in his voice.

Joey tossed her an answer: "Liv got stuck at her dad's, finishing off some stupid crumhorn or something."

"I might go over there," said Sheneel.

Joey gave her a blind look—he was really listening to Dalma, who'd started talking about what So-and-so had said to So-and-so today.

Timing was crucial; Sheneel mustn't hover there; it must look as if she'd always intended just to drop by and walk on.

Halfway to the old-town gateway, no one had called after her. She couldn't even hear their over-excited voices any more—there was only traffic, and birds in the park trees, and the breeze passing her ears, endlessly, arrhythmically changing the air around her.

| | | |

She was in the elevator with Lon. It was her third morning with him and her last. If she didn't ask him now, she'd have to do it in white time, with Rowan butting in, or in the canteen, when she'd be busy eating.

"There are rumours about people who work with white time," she said.

"Ah-huh. Wondered when you'd ask."

"About the travel perks."

"Yep." He pulled his eyes down to hers. She waited for something further, but of course he gave her nothing. *That's your answer: Yes.*

"You've done it?"

He nodded, his grey eyes drilling into her. She tried to think of a question that wasn't frivolous. "Where did you go?"

He kept drilling. "Lots of places. Or times, strictly speaking."

She wasn't big on history, herself. "Did you go . . . ahead?"

"Yup."

The way he was looking at her! Like, daring her to go on throwing these lumpish, gawky, *teen* questions at him. "How—" Her voice caught. "Hrm. How far?"

"Oh, a good long way," he said. His voice seemed to be getting softer. She wished she had a pip in, to hear him properly.

"Like, millions of years?"

"*Like*, thousands," he said. "No, not *like*. *Really* thousands. Really two thousand five hundred. Circa."

In her head she heard Dalma say, *Did you really? This is ultima cool! Wow! What was it like? Tell me everything!* She could *see* Dalma, in this elevator, hugging herself, stomping and grimacing with curiosity, asking and asking, *flooding* out questions.

But what do you ask this man, those eyes? He's on patches, for godsake—what did he see in that future? The elevator rumbled and shivered around them. She could ask anything—that was part of the problem. She couldn't ask a Dalma question, and she didn't know if she *had* any questions of her own.

"Were we there?" finally she said, in almost a whisper, horribly afraid. "People, I mean? Our kind of?"

He kept it up with the eyes. He swallowed. The elevator changed tone, whined down, stopped.

"Oh, people were there." He didn't move from the rail, even when the doors opened.

Sheneel looked to the opening and then back at him. His eyes were   dammit, she was so bad at this! Was he during her, pitying her, laughing at her? That wasn't a real smile, but the eyes, they had real stuff in them. His head was chock-a-block with it; he was ready, more than ready, to pour it out his mouth the way he was pouring it out his eyes.

"That's all," she said, in a little, light voice. Despite his eyes, she moved off the wall. "'t's all I wanted to know." And she walked past him out of the elevator.

| | | |

Now she was good at attaching the suction cups, using the moisture-patch at her belt and placing them where

Lon showed her. And she keyed in everything they told her, figure by figure—with only the vaguest idea of what each figure related to, although Rowan reminded her every time. But that was okay; she *did* it, without losing her cool, and capsules and creatures disappeared as they should. She tasted the occupation. She had hands-on experience.

This last day she did it all. Rowan told her everything, and Lon just floated at her elbow and watched. Twice she chose not-so-great spots for the intake cup. "You won't get a clear feed there, Sharelle," said Lon.

"Sheneel, Lon," said Rowan and she in unison.

"Looks like my job's on the line, Ro," said Lon, after the third entity had disappeared.

"Looks like it, Lon. She's got the touch."

Sheneel tried not to feel pleased. They were just bored and jollying her along; it would be childish to congratulate herself. "What's next?" she said.

Rowan reeled off sector and subsector coordinates, and the entities glowed near and far.

She dispatched a tiny capsule no bigger than her head.

"A DONNY," said Lon.

"You got it, Lon," said Rowan.

"What's a DONNY?"

"Whew," said Rowan, "what's a DONNY, Lon? You explain to Sheneel while I get you over to that flagellate thing."

"Dubious Or Not . . . not previously encountered or something. What are the other initials, Ro? Doesn't matter. Means it's new. Analysis will have to put their little thinking caps on. Here we are, Shania. A piece of string. Zap that."

With some difficulty, she did.

"Won't be needing me around much longer," said Lon. "Looks like I can retire now." Sheneel was getting used to his repeating things, too. She'd done it herself a few times.

Rowan spilled more numbers. Sheneel pointed her face towards where she thought he meant, and was gratified to feel the cable reorient her to face that way—the numbers were starting to mean something. She moved her shoulders to search with her chest-light. Something glimmered at her in response.

Then there was a loud hissing in her voice-pip. Through it, she heard Rowan swear. "Lon, what the hell?" The pip was dead of Lon's breathing.

Rowan's rushed in to fill the space, loud and fast. "Sheneel. I'm turning you to Lon. I want you to clamp hold of him with your legs and do whatever I tell you."

Lon spun into view. "What's happened? What's he done?" His cable was coming after him, the unsnapped end of it probing at his revolving middle.

"Grab him. You got him?"

She pincered Lon's knees with her legs. He didn't move. She couldn't see his face.

"The cable hole, Sheneel. Can you get the cable back in? You've got a little time with the reserve oxygen—heck, no you haven't! Why didn't I notice—What can you see through the cable hole?"

"Huh? Are you talking to me? Who are you, anyway? Where are we all?"

"*You* are Sheneel. *I* am Rowan. *Lon* is the man in front of you. *Look* in his cable port. What do you see?"

"Checks. Shirt. What am I doing here?"

"You're doing fine. Sheneel. Push the shirt aside. Output cup. Wet it on the belt-patch, Sheneel. Stick it on him. Stick it on Lon's skin."

"*Skin?* What—? I'm confused here."

"*That's* okay, Sheneel. *Out*put cup, Sheneel—*moisten* at the belt. *Lon's* cable port, Sheneel. See the shirt? *Pull* the shirt out, Sheneel. Ex*pose* some skin as quickly as you can."

Skin? This isn't skin. Purple-silver, and finely, finely pleated, like shrinking balloon-skin—Oh, a scar. The cup won't stick to it. I'll have to put it to one side—"It's on."

"*Stick* the—it's on? You're right! We've got him. Input this, Sheneel. Carefully."

She keyed and keyed. "This is a long calacku-curli-culication—"

"Seven, five. Repeat them back to me, Sheneel."

"'s, Sir!" And she keyed and keyed, until Lon snapped away, with a suddenness that made her reel and grope for balance, the suction cups flailing in front of her eyes.

"I'm bringing you in, Sheneel. Remember me? Rowan."

"Rowan. Rowan? *Rowan!*"

"I'm bringing you in. You see the door, Sheneel?"

"I see the door. Rowan, where is he? What's hap—"

"I'm bringing you in the door. You'll feel better there. It'll be all right."

| | | |

Sealed in the transition chamber, Sheneel found the tabs of her helmet by touch and tore it off. There was easily room. Something was miss—*Lon* was missing! She slammed herself against the black door. Her chest-light caught something—but only an entity, one of those streaky patches of vapour. What had happened? Where had she been?

There was movement at the other window, a crowd of green-smocked people. "Are they doctors?" she said dazedly.

"Yes. You'll have to stay in there, Sheneel, for transition."

"And is that Lon's feet?"

"Yeah. He needs a bit of work."

She watched the row of backs, the lowered faces. She thumped on the door and a face looked up. She made an asking face, and the woman put her hands together and looked up to the ceiling.

"She's saying *pray* for him? What happened? Tell me! Rowan? You there?"

"You'll be told. Don't worry. There'll be a counsellor—"

"I don't want a bloody counsellor! I want you, Rowan, to tell me, Sheneel, what I did, what went on, what you made me do!"

"Just . . . you shifted him forward a little, that's all. It's an . . . it's an Approved Emergency Procedure. It's written up on the wall here. I just read it off—"

"Procedure for what? How'd he come unplugged? How come no one *said* that could happen? How come no one told the *school* it was so dangerous? D'you people think you can—"

"No, no. Sheneel. Sheneel. He unplugged *himself*."

She stopped thumping the chamber walls. She stood waiting for the sense of the words to come through. "But he was always really fussy about seals . . ." She sat down with a thud.

"I know," apologised Rowan. "He just—it just happens sometimes. In the field."

She watched the doctors. They were nothing but green-coated backs. Rowan went off-line to manage other parts of the crisis; now only the music played in her head, aimless and tranquil and madly irritating. She snatched the pips out of her ears.

She could only wait until transition was over. This was the last time she'd be in here—she'd better take notes. She stood up and ran her gloved hands around the curved grey ceiling and walls. Really, it was like being inside a front-loading washing machine; she wouldn't be surprised if the thing started to spin. She went to the dark side and made her hands into blinkers against the glass; now she could believe that the chamber did spin, just slowly, that her legs were sliding up over her head, and down the other side, and up again, over . . .

A synthetic bell dinged softly. Transition was over. Sheneel turned and freed the heavy door and stepped out.

The doctors all had their backs to her. Their murmured conversation came to her as if through a pip:

Is there a wife I should call?

A wife? Lon's not married!

He's not?

Hell, no. Don't you remember his last little excursion?

Jamal wasn't here then. But they've got a few like Lon down in your southern reservoirs, haven't they, Jamal? Time bunnies?

Don't tell me—he went forward? How far?

Forty-five hundred-odd. That was the limit, then.

Aargh, that's nasty stuff. That's the Sect Wars. We lost a woman there; she came back, she was just tatters.

Lon wasn't much better. Caught in some crossfire. Put him

right off marrying, he said.

How come?

Women want children, he says, and then children *want children, and before you know it they're there in the fifth millennium, signing up for whatever battle did* him *over.*

There were indulgent chuckles all round.

Any next of kin, then?

Jamal, it's not that bad. She got to him good and quick, that girl—

And they turned and saw her, and started to speak too loudly, instead of slightly too softly.

"Just stretcher him up to Sick Bay."

"I've already called them."

The praying woman stopped rolling up fine cable and gave Sheneel a thumbs up. "Don't worry, love. Strong as an ox, is our Lon."

One of them still knelt beside Lon, holding his forearm. "Don't worry, mate," she was saying. "We all make mistakes. We've got you back, and that's the main thing."

"Yeah, for *you*," came the croaky answer.

Lon's suit was cut open neck to belt, chopped electronics trailing and biologicals leaking to the floor. They'd slashed open his check shirt; it lay sodden on either side of him. His chest was smudged with the pale-green sterile grease of some doctor-procedure, and moved without any rhythm that Sheneel could see.

She looked closer. One side of Lon's abdomen was chewed into detailed purple-and-silver knots. His chest was starred in several places with puncture marks the size of dollar coins, healed over shiny.

"Where's Sharelle?" he said.

"Sharelle?" said the doctor.

"He means Sheneel. That's me." Sheneel squatted opposite the doctor, and put her face above Lon's.

"He's just had a heck of a jolt," said the doctor. "Don't take anything he says too seriously."

"Ah, you," said Lon. "Yes."

Now, on top of everything else in his eyes, Lon had illness—body-illness, not mind. It didn't stop the eyes doing that thing they did, though—asking, speaking, meaning stuff. Expecting her to *see*, to *know*—and she didn't. She waited for him to tell her.

"I'm torn three ways," he said, then faltered.

"What do you mean?" said Sheneel.

"Between saying sorry and saying thank you . . . and saying bugga you."

God, he was so pale, so grey, so *old*. So different from the Lon that had sealed her into her suit this morning. So . . . storm-tossed, and small.

A tear went *tick!* on the wrist of her suit. Her head jolted up in surprise. "You don't have to do any of those things," she said. "I just happened along. I just did what I was told, whether it was a favour to you or not." Babble, babble.

He put his hand on her knee and her wet sleeve, so close to her face he could have just lifted a finger and touched a tear. "Don't get into this game, Sheneel."

Breathe. Sniff. "'kay. Like I would've anyway."

"Promise me—make it a promise."

"Okay, I promise."

"Because someone'll suggest it for sure, you've done so well. And your mind might change. Promise me *good*."

Green-clad doctors were moving in on her peripheral vision, with a gurney.

"I promise you good." It sounded like a joke, somehow—as if she were rudely imitating him—and she gave a little, uncomfortable laugh.

He didn't wink, or pat her knee and look away. He didn't crack any brave jokes, or say a neat goodbye. His eyes were warning beacons flashing darkness instead of light, and his hand was a stone hand.

Then they were lifting him, and he had to close his eyes with the pain. She stood back and watched him go, her heart thumping. For a second there she'd been a colleague, she'd been a fellow, and she wasn't ready to be the fellow of someone like that. She was too whole and healthy; she was too *young*—couldn't he see that? She didn't know anything!

They wheeled Lon into the elevator, and the shining doors rumbled closed. Sheneel stood in her white time suit among the milling doctors, blinking back tears, all trembly with shock.

| | | |

What was the highlight of your occupation-tasting experience?

〜

| | | |

Sheneel,

I was looking forward to a report that was <u>not</u> about the release party, so I'm a little disappointed that there's such a lot of white space in this account of what must have been an absorbing and varied occupation-tasting experience. Your impressions of visiting white time would, I'm sure, have been valid and interesting, *and I would have appreciated some insight into the scope and nature of the work undertaken at the Commonweal's lab—not to mention your feeling for the purpose and value of this aspect of the Commonweal's work.*

I hope your summer session on the program yields fuller results.

—Sir

| | | |

DEDICATION

"Today of all days, Harmon!" said Nella. She closed the door behind the palace messenger and turned to me, wringing her hands.

She was like this now, always anxious, always wanting me nearby. When we first wed, she was immensely sure of herself; at the twins' birth I had been cowed by her strength. But now she was much more like a child herself, often needing direction and calming. She followed me to my wardrobe. "Can you not plead busyness?"

"It's the king's daughter," I said. "Our children are only *our* children. The palace does not see them." I was a little flustered myself, putting on my palace clothes.

"Should we postpone our dedicating, then?"

"No, go on without me, Nella. I'll be as quick as I can. How long can it take to dress a motionless body that doesn't care how it looks?"

"But how does all *this* fit together?" She fluttered her fingers towards the nursery, the laid-out raiment, our babies only half dressed for their dedication at the temple.

"Call for my mother. She will know. I must be at the palace." And I left without kissing babies or wife.

As I hurried down the avenue, the day took on a strangeness like a birthing-day's. How could our princess be dead? Only a year ago I had been faithfully serving her, for those few dazzling months I spent as dresser under her wardrobe man Kinner.

"But Kinner has been ill," this morning's messenger had said. "His wife said the news itself might kill him, let alone the dressing of her. She says you will know what the princess liked, what will suit her."

"I will?"

"Better than any other. Be quick! She must be ready when the king returns. He is being summoned from the lake-pavilion even as I speak."

So now I was trying to hurry without perspiring into my best clothes, searching the princess's wardrobe in my mind. Something dark, something plain but fine . . . And the strangeness was in the air like the first autumn day without haze, a kind of terrible clarity.

Everything about the palace was subdued: all the pennants were gone, the flowers were stripped from the star-bushes in the portico, and people fell silent at my approach.

I presented myself to the door guard. "I come to dress the princess."

"She lies in her own chamber, Harmon. You may proceed there without guard."

So I entered the royal house, and walked there again, this time as a lone and competent man, a father and a robe-man myself, on call to the king-cousins. The passages and halls were familiar from my months at Kinner's heel, yet they too were changed by my time away. The princess's wing of the palace was musty and chill from being closed all these months; the rug underfoot felt slightly damp.

Two carry-men passed me, with meticulous greetings. Kinner and I had met the queen in this same passage not ten months ago, hurrying, distracted, already looking ill. "Kinner, have you seen my girl?"

"No, my lady."

She had whirled on past us, directing servants here and there. And when we reached the princess's bedchamber there had been no princess to dress. I saw neither mother nor daughter again; the princess had vanished from court, and the queen died of the grief of it two months later. I had heard that the king in turn was almost lost to us, so sorely did he feel the queen's absence, so great was his rage and bitterness against his only daughter. All the kingdom still lived under the shadow of it, though formal mourning for the queen was long done. That shadow could only deepen with today's news.

The bedchamber was dimmed, but even so I could see how bare and impersonal it now was. There were no clothes cast on the floor; the princess's hunting trophies, mounted heads and horns, had been stripped from the walls; the sprawl of books and papers was gone from her desk; and a crystal pen-holder and two fragile open-fans lay there, the sort of ornament the queen loved and the princess loved to scorn.

Two people conferred in whispers over the lidded casket, which lay on the floor. It was of plain flat-metal, the resin seal poorly applied and coming loose, the princess's name roughly painted on its paper label.

"Harmon, isn't it?" Tresor peered at me. He was one of the fussier housekeepers. "Well, you know what you're here for, man," he said. "Get to it—we've no time for maundering. The king has only to come from the lake-side."

The woman beside him flinched; it was Allyn, the princess's child-nurse. Her soft face was crumpled and dazed with simple grief.

The wardrobe was as I remembered it, still sweet with grass-sachets against the moths and tawny-beetles, the coloured robes graded exactly as they had been in my mind. I went to the darkest section to start my search.

As I moved the hung robes along their pole, I heard

other people arrive in the chamber. Tresor said, "Do it, then!" and there was the sound of tools against flat-metal.

I chose the robe the princess had worn for her majority, the first garment she ever had a say in designing. Oh, the quarrels there had been over that! She wanted it stark black, and gave way only as far as a dark, dark blood-crimson. She wanted it entirely without ornament, and was forced to assent to a closely beaded bodice, and leaf-work along the arms in a satiny crimson thread. She and the queen came to raised voices and almost to blows over the neckline, which the mother wanted ruffed and spiked, which the daughter refused to adorn beyond the braid edging the high collar. I smiled, the queen's furious face and the princess's stubborn one as clear in my mind as if they stood before me now.

Nails squeaked out of the casket rim in the adjoining room.

"Off with you, now," Tresor snapped. "We will do the rest."

"The lid will be quite heavy—"

"Out! You shall see nothing! Shoo!"

I heard the tool-men leave. I went to the chest of underclothing, opened it, and bent close over the folded beauties there, shining, scented, all intricate work and light, fringe and petal-border, woven and stitched with all the queen's love and ambition, to lie against her daughter's skin.

"Harmon?" called Tresor. "We need you in here."

I slowly straightened and went back to the chamber. The nurse had her hands to her mouth. Tresor himself looked a great deal less imperious than he had sounded, facing me over the loose-lidded coffin.

"Close the hall door," he muttered to the nurse. "You, Harmon, help me here."

I did as he bade me: I lifted one edge of the box-lid. So heavy, for such cheap metal! It must be lined with lead. We slid it until its weight tilted it towards me, affording Tresor the first view inside. The nurse turned from the door, gave a little mew and covered her face. Tresor became clumsy, and it was left to me to lower the lid to the floor. When I looked up, Tresor had placed shaking fingertips against his forehead, and was taking fleeting, fearful glances into the coffin. The nurse was weeping behind her hands.

Our lady had not had an easy death. One of her arms lay loose in the casket beside her, still sleeved in its fighting suit. One of her legs was missing from the knee down. The rest of her was caked mud and dried blood, with glimpses of fabric here and there, glimpses—quick glimpses—of flesh hacked, in some places through to the bone.

"At least—at least she does not give off a smell," said Tresor, his voice gone high and unsteady. "We had her brought straight from the battlefield, in the king's flying-ship—"

The princess's face, though uninjured, was dark with blood and dirt. It was expressionless as I had never seen it, not even for a moment. Only now did I realise how very full of passions she had been, our princess, how they had continually stormed across her features, rage clouding and laughter bursting out—only now, when they were gone.

Tresor controlled his ragged breathing. "I will leave her to you. Make her . . . make her easy for the king's eyes. Allyn?"

The nurse's sobbing abruptly ceased, and she wiped her face on her hood.

"There is not much time." Tresor went to the door. "I will post guard and messenger outside, and send you a more fitting casket. Cover her with a cloth before any enter—only we three must ever see her like this."

And he was gone.

| | | |

I had dressed and undressed this body many a time. And truth to tell, it was easier this day than on many others. The princess used to vent her resentment of court on us, twitching under our fingers as we adjusted strap and skirt-cloth, striding away before she was properly arranged.

Allyn the nurse washed my lady's face, slowly and assiduously, giving gentle moans now and again. When the princess's loose arm moved with my snipping away the suit sleeve, she covered her face and sobbed again.

I kept cutting, opening the rest of the suit. There were many scars on my lady's body from her training, and her filthy hands bore calluses and cold-boils. They were different hands utterly from the ones I had gloved for her majority ceremony. And the rest of her body—well, it was a different thing, too. All the softness had gone from it; all her curves had been starved and marched and battled into angles.

"How could the child do this to herself?" whispered Allyn.

I shook my head. "I never thought I would be glad that the queen is dead."

"Oh, yes—it's a blessing she never saw this!"

We covered the princess; the fine casket was brought in and the poorer one removed. Then Allyn and I lifted her onto the table, and Allyn set about washing the body while I cleaned the hair—and a poor, chopped tangle it was, to be soaped and rinsed and combed and perfumed.

Allyn paused often, overcome, in her sponging of the mud from the battered skin. "Ah, my baby . . . a bare fourteen and the cause of so much sorrow . . . an *axe* has been here, look!" Perhaps her weakness made me the stronger, or perhaps it was my long habit of adherence to duty, but I kept working, reverent but speedy. I was aware all the time of the king's drawing ever closer to us. How fast? Was he prostrate with grief on a litter, or hurrying, on horseback?

"Ah, but she is so ruined, who was so lovely!" Allyn cried out when the corpse was clean and dry before us. She was right; the princess still appeared soiled, with all her bruises and grazes. We had wrapped the larger wounds to keep the trunk and limbs shaped right for clothing, and the white bandages made her skin seem all the darker with injury.

"But she must not *seem* ruined," I said. "Not to the king. Fetch some powder, Allyn, and dust that bruise on her forehead."

I went to the clothing-table, and one by one I brought the many garments, layer over layer, that the princess would last wear. Allyn calmed once the first undershift was in place, covering the bandaged leg. And she helped me—she was strong-bodied and could lift the princess for my dressing.

This was not like dressing babies' small, rubbery bodies, guiding these heavy limbs into sleeve and under-skirt.

It was very much like the time my lady spent all one night stalking a skunk-cat in the ravines, and had to be bathed and dressed in her sleep for a midday feast the next day—only this time she did not moan or try to squirm away from us. She was so obedient!—in *this* was she most different. Those calluses, those many hurts, were only what one would expect of such a fierce and fiery girl once she had her own way, once she freed herself from soft palace living.

At last she was fully attired—the majority-robe and the two sleeve-layers beneath it held the loose arm in place. Allyn stood, awkward, holding one beaded court-slipper. The other was on the princess's only foot.

There was a knock on the door.

"Stay away!" I called out.

"I am to tell you," cried the messenger, "that the king's party has been sighted in the pass."

The nurse gasped and looked about, as if a foot might sprout out of nowhere for her to put the slipper on.

"Very well," I called.

"They are approaching with some speed," added the messenger.

"Very well," I said again. "We will be ready soon, tell Tresor."

"But we cannot just leave a *space* here!" hissed Allyn, shaking the shoe at me. "And the skirt—look how it falls where the leg is . . . is not there. He must not see that!"

"A roll of cloth . . . and a little one to make a foot! You tie up the hair." I hurried into the linen-store to find something suitable.

I had rolled the false leg and made the slipper appear filled, and Allyn had smoothed the hair back and fixed a knot of false hair behind the princess's head, by the time the messenger knocked again.

"The king is at the gate and coming!"

The nurse and I exchanged a frightened look. "She must be in the casket," Allyn whimpered.

"I will lift her. You hold the arm steady."

"But the leg—"

"When she is in the casket." And I took the body in my arms, and we walked around the casket and gently—gently but *swiftly*—placed and straightened her. Allyn smoothed wisps of hair back from the face. I fetched my rolled cloths and quickly did the leg and foot work, and I was just bringing the blood-crimson hem of the robe down to cover all but the toes of the glittering black slippers when—*thump!* . . . *thump!* the kingstaff struck the chamber door.

Allyn leaped away from the casket, cast a clean cloth over the wash-table, and kicked the muddy washing cloths behind a cushioned bench seat. I gathered up the combs and bowls and hair-oil bottles, and was hiding them there also when the door began to open.

Then I saw nothing but the carpet before my feet, as I stood beside Allyn in our deep bows to the king.

Several people entered—those would be the princess's five brothers as well as the king, and the king's close-retinue, those dour women and men with whom he had kept company since his widowing. There was a moment's pause, then someone strode towards the coffin. I straightened from my bowing to see the king, self-dressed in riding clothing, standing at his daughter's foot. He put back his head and uttered a keening cry. Several other people took up that weird sound—the nurse beside me began straight away. But something stopped me joining in, something in the king's face, some note in his voice. In the midst of the others' keening, he ceased his own noise, and walked up to his daughter's head, and bent over her.

My breath caught. Only I could see them, the live face and the dead. *Wake up, girl!*, was my thought—I wanted her face to be animated, and thus protected, against this look her father cast on her. For though his stance was hunched and broken as for grieving, no tear fell from him; instead, his eyes shed only the cold light of an immense satisfaction.

The keening ran and churned in the domed ceiling. The nurse was sobbing again, loudly now that it was proper, and she fell against me and I supported her. The king hung there over his daughter, his eyes bright, his gaze grim and greedy on her emptied face.

And then the reality struck me, like a lance down my spine pinning me to the floor. I had held my princess's severed arm, I had lifted and arranged her beaten head, I had carried her cold body in my arms. But only now did I truly apprehend that she had died— and died alone on a foreign battlefield, with her father's curse on her head.

The king straightened. Seemingly dazed, he walked towards his family and attendants, who put out their arms to him, who drew him in among them. He bowed his head as if overcome, and their keening intensified. They led him from the room, slowly, in deference to the grief they imagined he carried. The nurse broke away from me to join the entourage. And the princess lay, lone, still, beautified in her high casket, abandoned in her musty rooms by all but echoes of the court's wailing.

| | | |

I arrived near the very end of my babies' dedication ceremony. The celebrant had just taken a handful of blue-ash from the stone bowl and was pressing a pinch of it to my wife Nella's forehead, and to my brother Frand's, who was taking my place. My little boy Aitha and his sister Heely lay on padded cloths to either side of the ash-bowl, lifting their heavy brocade robes into disarray with their small, strong legs, spoiling the gold leaf-work of their cuffs with their mouthings.

Nella and Frand took up the babies for the final blessing. Frand turned, saw me at the door, and brought little Heely all the way down the temple to me. He pressed his forehead against mine to transfer the blue-ash, and gave me the baby.

I walked towards the celebrant. All around me was my smiling family, but I could not smile myself. Dead-hearted I was, yet I had never been so conscious of my child's weight in my arms, or seen so clearly the intertwining symbols carved into the arch over the celebrant's head, or felt so fully the holiness of a temple occasion. Awe hung in equipoise with the horror within me.

When Nella turned with Aitha she saw some of this. Her face changed; she looked freshly woken, curious as a bride. I touched her cheek as I reached her; I had so much to tell her.

But it would have to wait. I took my place beside her, and held Heely as Heely liked to be held, against my heart and looking over my shoulder. She explored the braid of my palace coat with her tiny, slow-moving fingers, her head striving for steadiness, her breathing light and never quite even.

The celebrant raised his arms and resumed his chant-ing, moving us all towards the high final point of the ded-ication. I held my baby daughter tightly, and closed my eyes to listen.

| | | |

TELL

AND

KISS

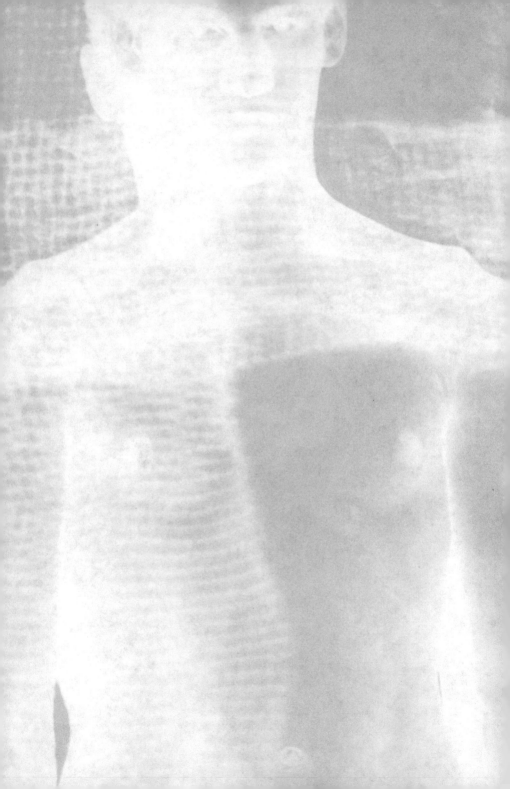

There was quite a crowd at the mouth of the arcade; first off I didn't see Chump. But then she turned to laugh at something Angel Lukovac said. Her face sprang out at me. She'd had a *serious* haircut—just now, just since school.

She saw me. "Hey, Rock!"

"Hey, Chump!"

"You still on for Clean-Up Day tomorrow?"

"Sure am."

"We're still a *team*?" She grinned.

"A team with a dream." Oh, I can quip, all right. I can come back with one-liners till the cows come home. They don't count; they don't shed any grams.

"Tomorrow, then." She was laughing at me. Maybe she could tell I *really* wasn't sure about the haircut. I felt shy of her new cheekbones, of her eyes, of her big smiling mouth. I was glad I was on my way to counselling.

Not that I was fat anymore; I hadn't been fat for over a year. But those are the rules: a half-hour of counselling and personal story every weekday for fifteen months post achievement of goal weight.

"Evan! How's my boy?" Gardi was in Reception, arranging flowers—from some svelte, grateful client, probably.

"Hi there," I said.

"How's it going with you, then?" She's pretty good—that almost didn't sound like a loaded question.

"Oh, along, you know."

"Uh-huh? Come in and tell me about it."

So in I went, the way I do; I sat down, I did the thirty minutes' chatting. Gardi was her friendly, easy, watchful self.

"You're a little impatient today, do I sense?" she said.

"I am?"

"You seem so. A little edgy, maybe?"

I blinked, shook my head. "I don't think so," I said. "I mean, I can't think what I would be edgy about." She was *regarding* me still, and I laughed. "I really can't. I'm not trying to hide anything."

"Nothing unusual happened today? No breaks from routine, nothing unsettling?"

"Nothing. Truly. I got up, I ate, I showered, I went to school. Nothing at school."

She nodded, nodded some more, all the time watching me. Let me off the hook with a twist of her head. "Okay. If you think of anything, I'm here for you tomorrow, too, Evan. You know that."

"'kay. Will I send Mike in?"

She smiled—sometimes she can't resist my sense of humour, even though she's supposed to be the serious all-noticing Story-Board-accredited counsellor. "Thank you, Evan. If you would."

"Hi, Stonehead," fat Mike Dargall wheezed when I hit Reception. He had a lot to get off his chest. And his belly, and his hips and his thighs. He had several extra chins to explain away. Even his fingers were loaded down. I was glad I was not Mike Dargall. I was near the end of my stint; I was nearly free to go.

I jerked my thumb over my shoulder. "She wants you, man."

"Oh, hold me back," he said wearily, and began the several-stage process of getting himself out of the chair.

I didn't stay to watch. Guys like Mike, I try not to. Who wants to watch people suffocating themselves in slow, slow motion?

| | | |

I could smell Dad's apple strudel baking from out on the street. He was cutting up potatoes into chips when I walked in.

"How was your day?" he said.

"Pretty average."

"Sounds a little automatic, son."

I looked him in the eye. "No, really, I've just been talking to Gardi about how average it was." Meaning, *I have a counsellor for this—I don't need it from you, too.*

He conceded with a nod. "Feel like a steak?"

"Bigger the better," I said—although for a flicker of a second I nearly said "No thanks." Bad habits die hard. I know it's got nothing to do with *food* how much weight you carry, but it just seems logical: the more stuff you put in yourself, the heavier you get—there's more *matter* to you. Well, it seems logical to a worried mind. Not that I was worried *now*, of course.

I did my homework in the kitchen, to keep Dad company. Whenever I looked up, Mum was looking down at me from the studio photos on the high shelf opposite. They were carefully posed and lit to make less of her weight: a hand propped her chin to cover the flesh there; she wore dark plain clothes, probably with corsets underneath them; the focus was sharp on her eyes and lips, with the bulk of her blurring away into the dark background. There was a photo for every year she'd been away—four in all—and in that time it didn't look as if she'd lost so much as a milligram. She wasn't telling anybody *anything*. She was a proud lady.

"Even for our sakes, Evan," Dad once told me, "she wasn't willing to compromise. 'Private is private,' she told me, 'and I don't care who knows I think that.' Quite a woman, your mother." And he couldn't help sounding proud along with exasperated.

The steaks hit the pan and hissed frantically. "This'll be ready in two shakes," said Dad.

I got up and turned my back to the photos, fetching out plates and cutlery.

| | | |

Chump was at the depot, gloved and ready for Clean-Up.

"I like your hat," I said.

She grinned. "Thought you would. It's specially dumb, for your viewing pleasure. Chicken's Ears, I call it."

It was the colour of camels rather than chickens, and made of some kind of stretchy felt, all pilled with wear, with felt-and-vinyl earflaps sticking up. It was a very Chump hat. "It won't keep the sun off. Your old hair would've been sun-safer."

"And phooey to you," she said. "You know me. Style is all." And actually she was wearing quite a neat T-shirt under her overalls. A girl T-shirt, almost, instead of her usual floppy cast-offs of bro Tiernan's.

"Let's *do* it, let's *do* it!" She hopped around while I was issued my gloves and bag and litter-grabber.

We'd assigned ourselves a big Y of streets between the school and our two homes, streets that seriously depressed us, they were so dirty. They were a bit of a walk from the depot. When the novelty of pinching each other with the grabbers had worn off, we slung them in our bags over our shoulders, for speed.

"So what's with the make-over, Antoinette Louise?" I said, to slow her down a little. I was thinner than I used to be, but nobody said I was fit.

"What? Oh, the hair, you mean? I just got sick of it." And she took off Chicken's Ears and tousled her hair all up. It flopped straight back; it was un-mess-up-able.

"It looks shinier. Did they do something to it?"

"Nope, just the chop. It's healthier hair down there, closer to your head. Hasn't been in the weather as long."

"And look, you've got a neck."

She laughed. "Hey, what was holding my head up all this time—magnetic levitation?"

"It's so white; you'll burn so badly."

She shrugged and pulled the Ears on again.

We got to the end of Coffey Street and set to work. We were thorough; well, when cigarette butts are on the Clean-Up list your eyes do *get* thorough.

We worked up the whole length of the Y-stalk, in among the warehouses, before we let ourselves take a break and look behind us.

"We should've done this anyway," said Chump, wiping her forehead with her glove-wrist. "We shouldn't've waited till Clean-Up Day. All this time we could've been walking along *that*."

"It is kind of beautiful."

She tore off a glove. "Phoor! Look what this thingummajigger's done to me."

The grabber had rubbed a red blister up on the side of her finger. She held it out to show me. For a second I thought I was supposed to *do* something about it—what, kiss it better? I scowled at it in quiet panic.

"Should I pop it?" said Chump. "Are you supposed to pop 'em, or be careful *not* to pop 'em?"

"You're supposed to be careful not to get 'em in the first place," I said, suddenly cranky with her. "Hold the thing a different way."

It was a long morning. We didn't say much, just picked and picked. The depot was holding some kind of competition for the weirdest piece of rubbish, but nothing here qualified—aged cardboard, chunks of polystyrene blown out of the warehouse yards, snack-food wrappers, a bazillion cigarette-ends.

"I will dream of this tonight," Chump said. "I'll close my eyes and see weeds and squashed Big Milk cartons and grimy Chunkit packets."

We met some other school people at the park on the end of Hitchin Street; we'd accidentally overlapped our areas, and so we only had to do half the work cleaning up the park.

"This park has never looked so good, fellers," said Bri Drury, plunking himself down across the path from Chump, who was sitting fanning herself with her hat. Her hair had been sweated flat; she clawed it up into wet spikes, staring at nothing, blowing out her lips, fanning, fanning.

"What d'you say, Antoinette?" said Bri.

"Hum?"

"Park look good, or what?"

"Oh, yeah." She stopped fanning and examined her finger. "It's a vision of loveliness." The blister was busted now—big and red with a lid of loose skin. I looked away.

| | | |

Boy, was I tired. And my head was full of rubbish. I peeled everything off and dropped it all, every piece, in the laundry basket, and stepped into the shower. I pushed my face into the spray and Chump's face popped into my mind, staring at nothing, her injured hand flapping the hat. Looking tired, too.

I soaped up; I felt filthy all over. Arms, underarms, face and neck, chest—

And then I felt it. Belly. Just a bit of belly. The faintest, faintest rumour of fat, around my navel, and like the first whisper of a gathering cloud above my hips.

Oh, man. I rinsed, I looked. I was imagining things. I soaped up again, and . . . yeah, definitely. Very quietly, I groaned and swore. I felt under my jaw, where it used to show first. I really couldn't tell; I'd got so blasé about the whole thing, I'd forgotten what normal *was* around there. Half-soaped, I stepped out of the bath, cleared the mirror, peered in anxiously before it steamed up again. Couldn't tell. Suspected. Feared.

I had a hard time getting to sleep that night. I lay there feeling my middle, over and over. Was it different? Was it all going to start over again, with the counselling, with all that weighing and worrying, the conversations graded to go deeper and deeper, all those people, not just Gardi, giving me anxious looks? I remembered the bad old days, when do-gooders would sit next to me on the bus. "Tell me about yourself," the worst ones would say, the really lean, gym-hardened ones in those wet-look suits. The ones who weren't so fanatical said things like, "Do you live around here?" or "What do you think the weather will be like today?" or "Does this bus go past the Story Board Building?" But it was still obvious—they were trying to *draw me out.*

I turned over and stared at the wall. I might end up like Mum, taken away somewhere so my body wouldn't signal to anyone: FAT IS OKAY. PRIVATE IS PRIVATE.

But at least she'd *known* what she was holding on to.

Everyone had known: it was Gordie, my little non-brother. She'd got big with him, and he'd died inside her, and he'd come out, but she'd stayed big. And the Story Board people had said it was okay, for a while, for her to hang onto the grief, but after a year or so she still hadn't slimmed down. And I'd started growing—not just puppy fat to fuel a growth spurt, but serious, sticky kilograms. *Even for our sakes, she wouldn't compromise,* Dad said, but really it was for *me*, for *my* sake, for *my* good, that she'd agreed to go to the Health Farms.

And I'd join her there, if I didn't work out where this little extra blob of me was coming from, what untold thing it represented.

At counselling, right at the beginning when you're in with all the other fatties, they get you to visualise. First they show you a video of your blood, and point out the yellow beads of fat floating among the good red cells. Then they get you to imagine Story Bugs whipping through the mix, gathering up the beads like marbles into a bag, tidying them away to your excretory organs. They get you to think of your body as this nifty little society, with you as the team leader, ordering the bugs around any way you want. This was the scary thing now, the feeling that the bugs had run amok, that they were charging around inside me scattering handfuls, armfuls of the rotten beads, gunking up my nice clean bloodstream, turning me back into a wheezer and a lumberer. I should tell someone about this right now. I should go and wake Dad up and empty this into his ears. I was only making it worse for myself, for him, for all of us.

Instead, I just lay there and *made* it worse, until I'd worried myself to sleep.

The phone ringing tumbled me out of bed next morning. It was Bri Drury, of all people. "Huh? What do *you* want?"

"Got a question for you, Stone."

"Oh?" I rubbed my eyes ferociously to help them stay open.

"You know that Antoinette Stilling?"

"Mmph?"

"Well, are you and her, like . . . have you got any kind of . . . like, are you going out?"

The sleep started to clear from my head. "When? I mean, we go out all the time. Why?"

"No, I mean, are you, like, *together*? Is she your girlfriend?"

"No!" Now I was awake. "No, it's nothing like that. We're just friends, not . . . girlfriend, no."

"You know, that's good," said Bri. "Because I was thinking, if I made any kind of, you know, any *move* on that girl, I didn't wanna be busting into any kinda . . . any kinda *arrangement* you guys might have, you know?"

"Right. Okay." My feet were cold. My free hand was wandering around my waist, pinching, pinching. "Well, I guess you don't have to worry about anything like that," I said slowly.

"Good man! Thanks, Stone. See you around, huh?"

I put down the handpiece and used both hands on my waist. Definitely. Definitely something.

Antoinette Stilling. It always surprised me that Chump had that other name, that it wasn't just another joke name between us.

I was cold all over now, and feeling slightly sick. This did not promise to be a good day.

"He *asked me out*," said Chump, chewing on an avocado and alfalfa-sprout sandwich. She gave me an impenetrable look.

"Yeah?" I pretended to be surprised. Then I changed tack, pulling my elbows in to my waist. "Actually, I knew that. I gave him permission yesterday morning." Chump goggled, all bright green eyes and half-chewed alfalfa. "He rang me up," I went on, "and asked me, were we, you know, an *item*."

"You *have* got rocks in your head. You're supposed to *protect* me from lunks like that!"

I gave an airy shrug. "Well, nobody told me."

"Aargh. Now he wants me to go to some *go-kart* place with a bunch of them. Like that would be a great way to spend my Saturday."

"You going?" I made the first crunch into an apple. It was a good loud one.

She pulled faces. "Hmm? *Go*-karts? Who can know?"

I slipped into Gardi's voice. "I think that would be a very appropriate activity, for a young person. Social, active, plenty of opportunities to externalise."

"Oh, cut it. What do you think *really?*"

I goggled at *her*. "What is this, do *you* have to ask me for permission, too?"

"I just wanna know what you think!"

"Doesn't matter what *I* think!" Chump shot me a warning glance. I checked to see if anyone else had heard. "It's you and him, isn't it?" I said more quietly. "Up to you two?"

"Well, I guess." She kept pulling Chump faces, thinking it over.

"And go-karts would be, well, something new," I said, feeling weak, feeling as if Gardi were speaking through my mouth, taking over my voice.

"Something new," said Chump, and pondered that. "I don't know, Rock. I mean, *Bri?*" And her face scrunched up again.

I was holding an apple that was gnawed away right down to the core—when'd that happen? "Well, Chump," I said, sending it on a smooth arc into a bin, "it's entirely up to you."

|　|　|　|　|

"And how was today?" Gardi closed the door and sat opposite me.

"Today was fine. I talked to Chump a lot, to Bri Drury, to my dad this morning."

"You look a little tired."

"Yeah? I feel okay." Then I remembered my late-night worrying. I should say something about that. *Actually, Gardi . . .* No, I couldn't face it. I didn't want things to change, couldn't face that super-calm air Gardi would start to exude: *Well, Evan, this is quite a serious concern, isn't it?* And her getting out the pinch-testers and the charts— I couldn't stand it.

"That's a nice shirt you're wearing," Gardi said. "Quite fashionable—if you don't mind my saying so." She was smiling—she knew my attitude to fashion.

"You like it?" I'd worn it because it was just the tiniest bit loose. I didn't think I was visible yet, but I wasn't taking any chances.

"It suits you. You should acknowledge these things. Remember how we talked, about the age you're at now, and how there's a lot of change associated with that?"

"Oh no—the talk about *girls*. Do we have to?"

She laughed softly. "Not if you feel it's inappropriate."

"I do. Inappropriate for me. Now. Yet."

"I just want you to be prepared, when those changes start happening—"

"I'll be prepared. You prepared me. *Dad's* prepared me—"

"Don't keep any important story inside. Let someone know. Your dad. You can even come back to me, if you want."

I nodded. Then I heard her. *Back* to Gardi? "I beg your pardon?"

She was smiling again. "I've got the forms here for your release from Youth-Tell, Evan. How do you feel about that?"

I gulped, and she laughed.

"Well," she said, "I feel you've done very well. That big blockage you were experiencing about your mother is under control—we understand the stress of that, don't we?, and we're not harbouring any untold grief or resentment towards Gordie. You're a healthy size and you offer story very readily. You can raise concerns without hesitating, and you can even perform the occasional Leap Without Looking, those spontaneous confessions that are so good for the body. I'm very pleased with you."

"You are?" Why was my stomach churning, then?

"I know it can be difficult to let go. But this program mustn't become a crutch for you. We talked about the transfer, remember? These next few weeks, you'll have to make sure you get everything out to Antoinette and your dad, those primary confidants. I have faith that you can do that. Do *you* think you can, Evan?"

"Oh. Well, I suppose I can. I've come this far . . . Are you sure about this?" I was sitting forward. The waistband of my pants was digging into me, just a little, just pressing a bit uncomfortably.

"Absolutely sure."

I watched her fill out the forms. I should stop her. I should tell her about the weight. Or it could all happen again.

But I didn't.

"All right," said Gardi, slipping the form into the Story Board envelope. "I'll send this off today. As from this moment, you're cleared from the program. Free to go."

"Well. That's wild. Good, I mean . . ."

"It *is* good. But just remember," she said, getting up, smiling for me to get up. "No person is an island, Evan. Any time you need to confide and your primaries fall through, come to me. I mean that. It's important for all of us. We don't want to be weighed down by *individual* issues, do we?"

She showed me out to Reception. "If I'd known, I would've bought you a bunch of flowers," I said dazedly. Through the glass dividers I saw Mike Dargall struggling out of the lift.

"Buy *yourself* some flowers, Evan," Gardi said with a laugh. "You deserve them. You've worked hard, and achieved a lot."

I have? "'bye then, Gardi. And thanks. This feels strange."

"Nice little Leap there. You'll do well, Evan, I'm sure. Goodbye now."

I lay low and ate almost nothing all week.

"You okay, boy?" said Dad on Thursday night. He was doing risotto al funghi; I was sitting over *Folktale Tropes Level 4*, droning answers to Exercise 4.11(b) onto the page.

"I'm okay." *It's the rest of the world that's screwed up.*

"You're slumping a little, that's all. And you've been pretty quiet, this week. This week of all weeks. I feel concern about that."

"You do?"

"A concern I think your counsellor would share."

I looked up. "So *she* thinks I'm okay to go off Youth-Tell, but *you* don't, is that it?" I meant that to be deadpan, but it came out all spiky with resentment.

My dad gave me the listen-to-what-you-just-said look, and went on stirring the rice.

"Why don't you do that in the microwave, like Mum used to?" I said. I took great care with my tone. "Then you wouldn't have to stand and stir."

"I like to stand and stir. It's good, soothing stuff after a day's work. And you know me and handmade stuff—hey, if it wasn't so hot, I'd stir it with my hand." He added some stock and gave me the smile he uses when he's self-conscious.

Something about that nearly made me crack: the picture of my dad plunging his hand into the boiling pot to make my dinner. With my snappish voice still echoing between us, suddenly it was kind of unbearable.

Youth-Tell teach you how to spot untold story. When you find your mind shying away from things, when your eyes skid off faces and you bite back thoughts as unsayable, when you *least* feel like talking, when just the *idea* of it exhausts you—that's when you should most talk, before habits establish themselves, before the stories turn into secrets and start stacking up. As they do, under your waistband, under your chin.

"Something *is* wrong," I said—not because the Story Board said I should say it, but because of the smile and the stirring. "I don't know what it is, though. But when I do, I'll tell you."

He stirred as if the rhythm was keeping him calm. "Maybe we could talk around it. Is it to do with getting off the program?"

"No, I don't think it is. I don't know, Dad. Let me think about it."

"Think all you want, son." Stir and stir. "Just don't forget to say, a little every day." That was one of Youth-Tell's cheesy slogans, murmured into the risotto pot there.

"I will, Dad," I said. "I'll try again tomorrow."

| | | |

Saturday I spent mostly in bed. I woke up, did the pinch test, turned over and hid myself in sleep. Around noon I got up and pulled on a tracksuit that was old and soft, from last winter when I still chose fat clothes, not believing I'd ever not need them. Hey, I was right, right?

Dad was in his office, catching up on some work. I went and leaned in the doorway, and he turned around. The sight of the tracksuit checked him a little, but he covered that quickly.

"Hey-ho," he said. "Out of hibernation? Ready to do the weekend thang?"

"I thought I was already doing it."

He didn't laugh. He was peering at me, moving his head around. "You look a little puffy around the face, Ev," he said. "You coming down with something? Is that why you slept in so long?"

"It could be, I guess." I passed a hand along my jaw. "Yeah, I feel a bit achey in the joints. A bit fluey, maybe."

"Hot lemon and garlic drink?" he said, brightening.

"You're the primary caregiver," I said, just to see him spring out of his seat and make for the kitchen. Just to stop him looking at me.

I kept him going all afternoon. I suggested some big housekeeping, and helped him with it, vacuuming and tidying and hauling bed-linen and floor-mats out to the wash. I emptied the big shelves in the kitchen and wiped them down, and wiped down all the jars and stuff and put them back, and got out the Kleen and shined up the silver frames of the Mum-photos. *Yeah, I remember you doing this, Mum. Always being on the move, too busy to properly talk.*

We were still going that night when the phone rang. "I'll get it!" I called out, the obliging son.

"It'll be Denny," Dad called from the bathroom, where he was transforming the basin into a thing of beauty. "Tell him the tennis booking's moved to Tuesday. That's all he'll want—"

"Is that you, Rock?" said an anxious girl-voice on the line.

"Chump? It's only Chump!" I called out to Dad, who was still shouting instructions. "Hi, how is it?" I said to Chump.

"It's . . . funny."

"Oh." I didn't know what to say. "Right. Funny." *Why don't you tell me about it?* I said it in my head, but it didn't come out my mouth. I put the backs of my fingertips up under my softening chin. "So."

"It was go-kart day today, remember?" It sounded as if she was having trouble getting her words out, too.

"Hm? How'd that go?" I sounded bland and bored. My hand moved down and along my waist.

"It went . . . well, there was . . . this horrible *thing* happened—" And then I heard some funny breathing, little puffs and gasps.

"Chump?" I said, in hardly a voice.

"Oh *God*, can I see you, Rock?" she said, loud and ragged in my ear. "Can you meet me midway?"

"Sure, but . . ." But I was all over sweat and house-dust and Kleen. "Give me ten minutes."

"Make 'em quick ones, okay? I'm cracking." And the connection clicked off.

"What's with you?" said Dad. I'd leapt into the shower and was lathering up fast.

"Meeting Chump."

"Yeah?" He waited for more.

"Yeah." I got busy rinsing.

I put on not-too-tight jeans, a stretchy old T-shirt and an open jacket. "See you whenever!" I called, going out the door.

The night air was cold in my damp hair, refrigerational down my front. I zipped up the jacket and strode. It wasn't far. I only had to round one bend and there was Chump a little way along under the streetlight, standing slightly hunched in her red-ochre dustcoat and the Chicken's Ears.

I made a voice-noise when I was in hearing distance. She saw me and took one sagging step my way. I went up to her and stood. She was all strange. She didn't bounce or jitter.

"What is it, Antoinette Louise?" I'd never seen her like this. My spine was a hollow pipe filling with cold water.

"A girl lost her hair," she said in a fragile voice.

What—this is all about the haircut?

"And part of her head," said Chump, looking up at me. Streetlight crept in the fuzzed felt of her hat. It spilled over to her eyes, slumped on the tears there.

"How?" I said. "What?"

"At the go-kart track. Her hair got caught in the wheel. It was really long. We'd only just got there. It ripped away, roots and—and skin and all. I saw it—" The tears broke, and she jerked her face aside.

I slid the hat off her head. "But it wasn't yours." Her hair lay flattened there. I pushed my fingers through the top of it to give it some air.

She stood like a long-suffering dog, staring at her own thoughts. "But Bri and the others . . . We'd just come all that way, and they weren't going to let it stop them. You know, having a fun time?"

I nodded, rolling her hat in my hands to rub off the smooth, slippy feeling of her hair, the heat of her solid head.

"So there's blood all over the place, and these guys trying, really carefully, to get the . . . the sca . . . the scalp off the ax . . . axle . . ."

I'd never seen Chump cry before. I felt sick; I was all gooseflesh. She stood, hands in pockets, and sobs came out of her as white puffs of air.

I remembered being little, and Dad sitting crying on the couch after Mum went. I hadn't been sad myself; I'd just wanted Dad to feel better, to be properly with me. I remembered the clean, serene feeling of knowing exactly what to do, and I did now what I'd done then. At least my arms were long enough now—they went right the way around Chump.

She sobbed into my shoulder, shaking. My left ear was half-frozen; my right ear was warm against her hair.

She recovered a little, dug her chin into my shoulder to talk. "And Bri's sitting in a go-kart, tapping his fingers on the wheel. 'Someone get me going here? Come on, Antoinette, give me a push-off?' Like it's a big *joke*, with this girl moaning, and everyone—" She buried her face in my chest and started shaking again.

"It's gross," I whispered. "That's gross behaviour."

She nodded emphatically into my neck. "Terrible people!" she squawked. "And I knew it! Why'd I go? Why'd I ever say yes?"

She pulled herself back from me. The cold air leaked down between us. I was mindless; all I wanted to do was pull her close again. "What did *you* do today," she asked fiercely, tear-smear all around her eyes, "you and your dad?"

"I slept in. He worked. We were cleaning up the house when you called. We didn't do anything."

"You see, I would rather have *done* that kind of nothing." She sniffed hard, and shook me a little to convince me.

"I would've rather you would've, too—I mean, I'd have liked you to've—"

Her lifted face stopped me, my old mate Chump, but too close for mateship. Close enough for me to see the wet spears of her eyelashes, the way her pupils shrank and then opened as she read my face. Close enough to make me dizzy. "I wish you had, too," I managed.

"Do you really, Rockhead?" She had her own voice

back now, straight and clear and low.

"I really do." *My* voice was gone, but I was getting words out. "Fact," I whispered, "you can come home and sort out my laundry *now*, if you want."

She spluttered a laugh. "In a minute," she said. "In a few minutes, maybe." And she slid her cheek onto mine and held me tightly.

I swear, as I stood there wrapped around Chump, I could feel those Story Bugs at work, plucking up fat-marbles and stowing them in their sacks, busy-busy, the merest tickle under my chin and around my waist. I could see, by the streetlight, that cleaned blood streaming lean and rich and red through my eyelids; I could feel, just behind my lips—my lips on Chump's warm head, tickled by Chump's hair—unspoken story swarming on my tongue, getting itself ready to be told.

| | | |

THE

QUEEN'S

NOTICE

He hurried ahead to the queen-chamber, his jaws aching from the fight. The colony was still reeling from the attack; cousins boiled past and over him with only a quick trace, a chirp or a slight hiss. But he had mission and message; they gave way to his shoving, even those larger than he.

The chamber's air was steamy with young. Servers ran about, collecting the ripe young-beads for the compost-chamber. The queen gnawed fresh sweetbulb as the young fought and fixed themselves to her teats. The scent here was absolutely true; it cleared his head of anything but loyalty, and he abased himself. The queen lifted her face from the bulb and sniffed, and gave a trill.

He was dazzled for a moment—then his fellow-fighters jostled from behind, and he remembered his mission. "It was the sun-start mob," he panted. "They came in several ways at once."

"Dybbol," came her slow voice. "I know you."

"They are gone, sweet queen. You and the young are safe. We blocked all five tunnels that way, and none penetrated."

"That red-snake last summer. You were the one, weren't you, who turned that back?"

"Among others. We always serve our queen. We always keep the colony."

"Ha," she said, and there was more gnawing.

Hunger surfaced in Dybbol's stomach, now that he was no longer saviour. Behind him, some fellow's insides gave a muffled skirl. They were ready to leave.

But the great queen stirred. The young protested, falling off and lolling on the chamber floor. "Come here, Dybbol," she said. "I am all weighed down by our future."

He pushed the sweetbulb aside and there was her

face, warm and curious, her smell piercing his skull like incisors of pure sunlight. Confused, he abased himself and retreated.

Behind him, servers and fighters were twittering. "Stop your gabble!" the queen shrieked at them, rearing up. "Bring me food! Attend me, and fast! Come here, Quinnink—I will bat your eyes out for uselessness!"

With his fellow fighters, Dybbol forced a way through the dithering servers. Out in the passage, other smells reached them—pantry was best, and they followed that upward. Hard fighting always made them hungry.

At their head, Dybbol met Amkarra, and made ready to lock teeth with her as always.

But she gave no fight. "Hunh?" he said. "Why do you back and abase yourself?" He pursued her down a side-tunnel. Behind him his fellows flowed on towards pantry.

"I serve Her-Madam. I keep the colony," Amkarra muttered.

"Lock with me! Give me your teeth!"

But she put down her face and would not engage.

"Come at me!" He batted her stupid head.

She muttered into her paws.

"Tell me, then—why be abased?"

"You have Queen's Notice all over you," she said, and backed further, and somehow turned herself in the narrow space, and fled.

It was true, he did smell, strongly and cleanly of deep earth and queen-favour. His mind was beginning to fill with other things, as a quick-tunnel trickles full of loose earth, but he still had the queen's scent in all his skin-folds, creeping in his mouth-hairs, raw and clear, warm and sweet.

But pantry called, and company, and he went to answer both.

| | | |

He could not find a good fight. Whenever he closed his jaws on someone, they only lay limp. If he took hold and dragged, no one braced or threw their weight. No one would lock teeth and rock with him; no one would bat him back.

So when the beak-snake came, he heard it a long way off; he raised his head before anyone, and was the first one up the best tunnel and blocking. Dig and dig and dig—he sprayed the hard, smooth snout of the thing with earth as it came on. It bumped against the blocking mound, and he felt a flicker of its tongue as he closed the passage, closed out light and snake. He was all fervour and favour, nose to nose with the queen's enemy; he scraped and tamped, while the others hung back and trilled.

"I must save us alone?" he grunted.

Amkarra came forward, and could not stop abasing herself. "A true scent breathes from you," she said. "You have become too beautiful to fight beside."

"Bah. Go and report, then."

"Oh no," she said, and the others twittered, too. "Her-Madam will want *you*."

He knew that. It was new, but it was true. He hurried away, trailing the clean, strange smell of his own bravery.

| | | |

The young were days livelier, beginning to speak and close their jaws on each other. The queen lay almost as if dead, weak from their constant feeding. Beside her lay a bulb so fresh that Dybbol went straight up and secured a bite of it before he reported.

"Ah. You. Bold one," murmured the queen. "What do you bring me?"

"Another victory, queen below us all, heart of all our hearts." It was his gullet speaking, so grateful for food after fighting.

"Against what?"

"Snake, coming from sun-end as they all do, hot with light and hunger."

"And the size of it?"

"Bigger than any before, Your-Madam. Stronger than twelve cousins. Only speed saved us."

The queen gave a purring sigh and raised her head. "*Your* speed, Dybbol?"

"Among others, all our queen." Dybbol made to leave.

"Linger!" cried the queen. Her breath flew at him, cleansing him of hunger and care, and he was there before her, their muzzles touching, her scent locked bright in his head. Deeper in the chamber her immenseness moved against the spilling pile of young. He knew what to do, knew even though it was new: he must go to the far end of her great spine-arch. A scent was coming from her there, that spiralled higher and sweeter in Dybbol's head than any other ever, a scent that beckoned, that dragged him from her muzzle—

Sharp teeth caught in his haunch and flung him against the wall, knocking all scent from his nose. Servers ran anxiously about; young cheeped and squirmed.

The queen shifted. "Now is not yet the time," she breathed.

"The time?" He tried to shake his head clear.

"When these Two-Dozen disperse," she said, "that will be your time." And she pulled the bulb towards her and was gnawing.

He hurried away, dizzy with favour. Near the pantry, he met Barraud, one of the queen's two paramours. Dybbol did not give way as he should; instead, he reared and gaped, roughing the air in his mouth-hairs. Here at last would be a fight! Oh, and he was ready—he was unafraid even of a paramour today! He hissed and went forward—

—and met nothing. He fell to his paws. Barraud was gone off-side, two tunnels along.

"Aargh! Face me! Come at me!"

"I will not," came Barraud's trilling. "You are all over favoured and must save yourself for Her Immensity!"

"I am not *so* favoured," cried Dybbol, pursuing. "Come, I must put my teeth in something!"

"Not me!" Barraud sped ahead, threading through tunnels, forcing cousins aside. "I will not fight a favoured one!" came back faintly.

Dybbol began to lose him to the weaving tunnels, to the earth—and to a strong scent of alarm, souring the tunnel-mouths to one side. He veered that way, the scents showing place and activity and size-of-danger on the colony-map in his head—in two places. Two different dangers. He made, fast, for the digging danger, which was farther but greater. A snake would only take one fighter, then would leave; a digger might want several, might dig deep, might uncover the colony's heart.

"We serve," he panted, turning into the dangerous

tunnel. "We serve our queen. We keep our colony."

The tunnel was loud with flung earth and the snouting and clawing of the danger. Others were there, behind those doing the blocking. "Let me by! Let me help save Her!" cried Dybbol. But cousins braced themselves there, several clotting the tunnel. "Let me through! Make way!"

"We may not," they said. "Sniff yourself, man—smell how favoured you are now! Save yourself; we have plenty of warriors."

"Myself? But we must save the queen!"

"We have plenty of brave. Run along and eat, and save up your strength."

Dybbol turned back. His whole body swam with energy against the danger; his teeth ached to lock, his jaws to dig hard earth. He went to pantry and found a good rock-root, the biggest there and the hardest. He wrenched it out of the pile, and the pantry-wardens let him pass with it, making no murmur.

He gnawed and chawed all that day in a side-chamber. All the colony's doings came to him on the breezes past his nose, in tremblings and skitterings transmitted through the earth to his sensitive paws. No one called him, to watch, to work, to *anything*. He crouched, he ate, he slept—in daytime, slept! And in the night ventured to pantry again, past his fellows heaped in corners, their warmth cupped in the dormitory chambers and trailing down the breathy tunnels. And Dybbol gnawed, and slept, and gnawed, and listened to the colony all around him—its vast, safe busyness so wonderful—and slept . . .

. . . and woke to the queen's screaming. "Arraaaagh! Where is my-bold-one-my-Dybbol?"

He was fear all through, a throbbing thunder of it.

The queen's voice caught him low in the spine and spread out from there. He sensed her turning in her chamber deep below, shoving her cousins away, shoving her cousin-cousins harder, roaring and shrieking. *The young are not in the queen-chamber*, the echoes told him. And not long afterward, *The cousins also are cleared. Her-Madam awaits you.* And the smell of the queen's greatest need, wild and sweet, spread through the colony. It crept into Dybbol's chamber and caught in the few outer hairs he had, around his nostril-folds, and clung there like thistle-fluff. He batted his own nose with his paws; he pressed his face into the earth wall, shaking all over.

Fighters came for him. He reared, he gaped, he hissed, frantic. There were too many of them.

"Come, now," said Barraud, "No one can escape the Queen's Notice." And they dragged and shoved him, struggling, from the chamber. "Good man," said Barraud. "Fight all the way. Make yourself delectable." For the first time Dybbol's head-map of the colony failed him. He did not know where he was, only that the queen's need was strengthening towards him, winding its tingling tendrils into his spine, spinning terror out of his loins as mean and hot as snake-breath.

Then he was there, wrestled into the chamber by paramours and fighters. He tried to scrabble out, but they were digging, flinging earth, trapping him there with the roaring queen—

—who fell silent; who loomed up and clouted him to the floor with her great paw; who stood over him, lust-breath whistling in her mouth-hairs. And humming in his jaws, boiling along his body, moving his nerveless paws for him was that fierce, new, intensely sweet scent that twirled out of the queen, behind.

| | | |

He dreamed he was young again, in a heap of young, inter-leaved with cousins. He chirped weakly, and they shifted, and their warmth intensified against him, pulsed him softly back to sleep.

He woke in pain, from nose-bristle to tail-nub—and alone, in a chamber too small for a dormitory. The only sounds were above him.

Amkarra came in, rolling a new-cut sweetbulb.

"Where am I, Amkarra?" said Dybbol. "Where is this chamber?"

"Why, right by Barraud's, of course, along from our Deepest Heart." She pushed the bulb towards him. "This is for you."

He found a feeble voice. "Enjoy it with me, cousin."

She put down her face. "I may not, bold one, queen's paramour. But I hope it fills you as your children fill the queen, for our colony's prosperity."

"For our colony's prosperity . . ." He lifted to the bulb a paw that shook with weakness.

Amkarra abased herself and backed away down the tunnel. Dybbol felt her go, her earthy fighter-smell fading under his own sweet reek. Then the fresh breath of the sweetbulb asserted itself, and he turned from the tunnel and began to gnaw.

| | | |

BIG

RAGE

Where am I? I'm all in a sweat, but the air on my face is cold. My head's jammed up against a bedhead, my heels are pressed hard against a footboard. Wherever I am, I'm totally alone—a mixed feeling, a kind of horrible relief.

Is that moonlight or dawn-light bunched in the curtains? The rabbit-patterned curtains—ah. A mind-gate clicks open and memories roll in, of the rainy, steamy, sick-making bus trip down here, of walking the gravel verge past the closed-up beach-houses, of pushing through the rainy garden to Bunny Cottage, where we kids always used to sleep in the holidays, daringly apart from the main house. I must have lain down in my clothes and passed straight out.

Blink, blink—my eyes feel fried and then dried. I get my watch to my face: four o'clock. If I were at Mum and Dad's I'd be sneaking outside with my mobile to make a pathetic, weepy phone call right about now. Shivering at the bottom of the garden: *What's happened to us? I love you, James, I love you*, trying to get the words to mean something, to be instruments for fixing things. Which they never were—that's why I'm here, to stop myself trying that stuff. Just to stop everything, and think for a while. "Because if you don't watch out, you'll get yourself committed," my sister Marnie had warned me. "I mean it, Billie—you're turning yourself into a crazy-girl."

Well, there's no point pretending I'll sleep any more. I push the quilt off and the wintry air bites down on me. I pull on my woolly jumper and my parka, and my chilled boots that are dull with rainwater. My brain's about to grind into gear again, and this room's too small for all that churning machinery. Any room's too small.

I go out, closing the door behind me. The rabbit doorknocker gleams brass-yellow; everything else is grey. Out the back gate. Into the dunes, the path pale under the scrub, whiskery marram grass leaning in from the edges. My feet feel over-protected in the boots—the air should be hot, my feet should be bare on the sand, I should be a little kid with a towel over my shoulder and cousins all around, hurling ourselves through the sunshine for a swim.

The beach opens out, same old long curve, Dog Head Rock crouched at the north end, the sea washing and washing. The half-moon's low, and a few fat clouds trundle across the stars—heaps of stars, heaps more than I ever see at home. They look three-dimensional, layer after layer going back and back forever, following some rule-system that's too huge for my raggedy brain.

I stump off to the south, where there's nothing to stop me, ever, if I don't want to. I veer down the beach to the harder, freshly washed sand, and put my boot-prints there. My teeth are clenched grim, as they always are lately; my fists push hard into my parka pockets.

I try to walk myself into a daze. I walk the moon down into the sea, walk the black sky grey, but my brain won't shut up. It keeps replaying all those conversations, all those humiliating things James said, all my angry come-backs that never seemed to hit the mark. On and on it goes. I'm so *bored* with it, and so *frightened* of it, and so cut to ribbons inside, and it's never going to be fixed, and even getting this far away hasn't helped—

"Just *stop*, why don't you?" I shout at the sea. "Just shut *uuuup! Aaaah! Enaaaaarf!*" And I stand there for ages, just bellowing into the noise of the surf, until I feel, not better exactly, but a bit emptier, a bit off-loaded.

Then I turn north, and stomp out my own prints one by one up the sand.

I'm nearly back to the house when something calls my gaze to the dunes, something darker than dune shadow: a big man, flung there on his side, head to the sea, legs splayed up the dune.

I could walk on; walking on would be the sensible-est thing for a girl on her own to do. Instead I stand there for a while, watching him for movement. It might be okay; he might be dead. I should at least see if he's breathing? Slowly I walk up the softer sand.

A man in armour. Seriously big. Long, dark, filthy hair in a spray across the sand. I crouch on the dune, trying to see whether his back's rising and falling.

Maybe he drank too much at some costume party and wandered down here to sleep it off. It's a good costume, look at the hand there, the overlapping plate like fish-scales going down the fingers. It must've cost him a for-tune. But where's the party? I didn't hear anything in the night.

A sudden snarling groan breaks from him—I fall back with a whimper into the cold sand. Embarrassed, I get into my crouch again, ready to run if he rears up and comes at me.

With a horrible scraping of sand on metal, he turns over. He lets out a shout of . . . pain, surprise, anger? I hold still, my heart drumming hard, my eyes wide.

Darkened sand is caked down his side. Through it, at the middle of it, dark fluid squishes out. Oh, my God. The hand that was underneath him stretches out towards me, dark all over with dried blood, the shaky fingers shiny red.

This is ambulance material. Phone nine-one-one.

But there's no phone. Marnie confiscated my mobile at the bus stop. "You don't need that. The last thing you need is that." So I'll have to run up to the shop. But you're not supposed to leave an injured person, are you? So—

Ah, he's looking at me! He's turned his head, and now his pale eyes—pale irises in *red* whites, far out!—are locked on me. All of a sudden it would be a Big Thing to get up and walk away. I can't quite do it, right at this moment.

He says something. His voice is used to bellowing, but he's trying to talk softly; the sound breaks up and mixes with the wash of the sea.

"Beg your pardon?"

He says it again, adds something more. It's not English. And not *dottore*, or *ospedale*, or anything I recognise from Year 9 Italian. I watch his lips. Total, nonsensical—and look at those teeth! Sheesh! It looks as if someone's tried to ram, I don't know, an axe handle or a spear butt in there, and knocked a couple of teeth out of his upper and lower jaw. He's looking rougher and wilder by the second—if it weren't for the voice I'd be out of here, off at a run, wound or no wound.

He starts to ease himself onto one elbow, talking at me, keeping his eyes on me so I'll know we're in this together. I get a better look at his face in the first sunshine. It's not pretty. The pain, a skull-face, comes and goes behind his real face, which is weathered like a surfer's or a yachtie's, with a flattened nose like a gangster's. It's hard to tell how old he is.

My own face starts to shake, it's been held so long in this anxious wince. I want to leave, I don't want to be here. I feel so *not* able to deal with this.

But if I don't, who will? Am I going to let the guy bleed to death out here?

"I guess, if I can get you back to the house . . ."

He's just so bloody massive—piece by blockish piece he lifts himself upright, and I don't know how he can do it, and I'm kind of laughing wondering how I can be any use to him at all. But when that big, armoured hand crunches onto my shoulder I'm not laughing. Right then I realise that (a) this can't be done, and (b) this can't *not* be done—if he slumps down again, he won't be able to get up a second time.

And so I turn superhuman. There's no way I can manage this, but I just do. We must look like a pair of drunks supporting only half his weight makes me weave almost uncontrollably on the cushiony sand. Not to mention the stink of him—not drink, but blood (I didn't realise blood *had* a smell) and also that terrible smell derelicts get, of long-ingrained dirt, with a dash of urine. If it *is* a costume party he's from, he's a little too authentic for my liking.

The beach is empty—where's a jogger, when you want one, an early-bird surfer? I'm boiling hot again; I've got this big floppy man-hand making blood-prints on the front of my parka; my *neck* is going to *snap*; and all the while this guy is mumbling—possibly singing, but that might just be the language—and puffing like a steam engine beside my ear, and how are we going to manage that little dune path side by side?

Well, we trample a lot of dune-preserving marram grass, is how, and damage a lot of replanted natural flora, and get very wet with shaken-down raindrops.

In the porch of the beach-house I prop him against the wall so I can unlock the two doors, screen and main.

He starts to slip almost straight away, and I work super-fast so I can duck back and dive under him on the bloody side and catch him. "Or I'll *never* get you up!" I gasp. His weight fuses every vertebra in my body, bows the bones in my legs, threatens to crush my collarbone. His great *rock planet* of a head droops forward as he goes unconscious; the doormat slides out from under me and my feet paw for a better hold. God, all this metal! My hands slip on the sandy chest-pieces as I try to hold him up, push him off me. He jerks awake again. A big gout of blood from his side splashes down my jeans-leg. I have serious doubts we can make it indoors. He's got bad shakes, and his eyes keep swimming upwards.

Scattering sand and blood, we stagger into the dead beach-house; the air's cold and smells of mildew and perishing rubber. I take him straight across to Marnie's room. "Finally! Made it!"

He half lowers himself, half falls, onto the bed—which suddenly looks flimsy, the jazzy floral mattress cover wildly frivolous. He breathes hard, his eyes closed, his face pale. The room fills up with the smells of him and I go to the window.

When I've finished wrestling with the lock and the runners that have lost their glide, he's got himself sitting. His head kind of wanders on his neck, and he tugs at the fastening under a shoulder plate with a shaky hand.

I have to get the armour off him. It takes *forever.* This isn't a costume-hire costume; it's some kind of authentic re-creation, each plate carefully laced to a reinforced leather shirt underneath. One plate's damaged on the edge, near the wound at his waist, and the leather underneath has a neat, round hole in it. Then there's a holed shirt made of some kind of hand-knitted metal, very soft and jingly and heavy, and then an undershirt, the dark grey weave clogged with old dirt—and a body smell I don't *believe*. My *eyes water*. I have to breathe through my mouth.

I peel the shirt off his shoulders. His whole top half is kind of comic-book massive, big chunky muscles like rocks under the skin—and they're not even flexed or anything. James jokes—*used to* joke (past tense, remember)—that he had a greyhound's physique, strong but lean and finely built. Well, this guy's your bull-mastiff, your monster Rottweiler, one of those dogs you'd be afraid would just casually take a child's head off like snapping at a fly. But the skin—I thought it'd be as weathered as his face. It's young, though. He's maybe even as young as me, but with, phew, what a different life behind him. Whole different kind of person from me *or* James. From anyone I know.

I can't get the shirt right off; all around the wound it's stuck to him. "What I'll do," I say, looking fearfully down at it, "I'll get some water to soak it off, hey?"

He looks up at me blankly, drunkenly. Then he pulls a horrible snarly face—*Oh no, this is where he dies on me*, I think—and with a yell that smacks me back against the wall he *rrrips!* the shirt off the wound.

"Far out—you could've given me some bloody *warning*!" I twitter.

He sags forward, elbows on knees, head hanging as if he's waiting to be sick.

"No-no, I don't think so. Not that, too." And I get down and hoist one shoulder up so he falls sideways onto the bed. His leg comes up, too, reflexively, to stop the wound stretching, and he lets out a string of what are probably swearwords, his voice deep and guttural, his face all bunched up. I'm glad he's incapacitated, or I'd be mincemeat.

I drag the other leg up onto the bed, and look at the boots and the metal-knit trousers. Still mouth-breathing from all the other odours, I think I'll leave these on him for the moment.

Then I give his belly one quick glance. It's overrun with wet and dry blood from the small, serious mess in his side. Oh, God. I'm not one of those nurse-y type girls.

"Yeah. Water," I say.

There's a lot of cleaning to do—so much blood, dried in layers on him. I go through four big bowls of warm water, squeezing blood out of the washer over and over. The wound keeps oozing blood as I clean it, slow and dark, and a bad smell comes out of it—not intestinal, but kind of sour, smoky, *unnatural*.

"You're going to need help with this," I tell him. "Some stitching, some . . . treatment. Doctor," I say clearly to his uncomprehending eyes. "Hospital. *Dottore? Ospedale?* I'll have to go into town and get help. I can't fix this." I try to show him with gestures. *Non capisce.*

I bend anxiously over the wound. "Nas-ty."

He mutters at me. Then he touches my head, and when I turn it he pinches my lips closed with his shaky, blood-smelly fingers. He wards off something with his other hand—those people I waved in a moment ago. His pale eyes give off energy at me, warning or fear, I can't tell.

"Yes, but . . . this?" I wave my hands over the wound. "You'll die of this without—"

He thumps his blood-black hand onto my shoulder, and says something very slowly, digging in the air over the weeping wound.

"Huh? Well, it's as clean as I can get it, you see. I've got all the sand out and everything . . ."

"Graachh!" He wrenches his head off the pillow, searches the room and waves a hand at the crumpled heap of his shirt on the floor.

I fetch it for him. "But you can't go out like this. You can hardly *move*."

He bundles it under his side. Then, with his thumbs, he pulls the wound open. My head jolts back as if he kicked it. With a long, low, grating growl he digs two fingers into the opening, two big man-fingers up to the knuckle, and works on something inside. I'm hovering over him, holding my head, wringing my hands, making feeble sounds; I think I'm going to be sick. His eyes roll in his head and he pauses, big rough breaths going in and out of that flattened nose, his working fingers swimming in blood, all his other fingers shuddering. Sweat has sprung out all over his arms and chest and face; it's running into his sand-filled black hair.

Then he hauls something out of himself, something small and hard and slick with blood. He holds it out to me, his face glowing with . . . triumph? Hatred? Relish? I take it in jittery fingers, my scalp crawling.

I rinse it clean in the water bowl. It bubbles underwater, and keeps up a soft hiss when I take it out. It's halfway between a bullet and an arrow, a battered silver cone with four sharp fins sticking out the sides. Specks of greenish-white froth are building from tiny holes at the fin-tips, giving off that poisonous burnt-out smell. "That's a mean thing to have inside you," I say, to stop myself from gagging. I lay it gingerly next to the bowl on the bedside table.

The guy lies in a faint, then, pretty much. I fetch him some water in a glass with a straw. He has a little difficulty working out what the straw is for, but he drinks the lot.

"Eight-thirty. I'll go and buy us some food." I sign it to him. "And a covering for that," I add, pointing to the folded clean dry washer lying on top of the wound.

He doesn't move or grunt, just looks dazed, so I leave. I change into clean jeans in Bunny Cottage, grab my wallet, head north up the beach to town. I buy some fat bandages and antiseptic powder, plus the ingredients for a good, solid, stewy soup involving pasta and vegetables and thick-cut bacon, and proper crusty bread for alongside. It feels very odd to be out here in the clean, modern world after having been up to my elbows in blood and sweat all morning. I guess getting up before dawn doesn't help a person's sense of what's normal.

I've just turned home along Anzac Street when I think I see a knight in armour crossing the road up ahead. I blink and he disappears, into the park. A minute later a car pulls up at the same spot, and two damsels get out, in shiny gowns, one's pale blue, the other's crimson. I speed up—I get this weird feeling they'll stop existing if I let them slip out of sight.

But I get to the park and there are dozens of them, damsels and knights and people in cloaks. There's a marquee set up at the edge of the park. There are horses with fancy cloths covering their heads. I stop at the gate and stare at them all.

One of the ladies setting up booths calls out to a friend, "Were we lucky with the weather, or what?"

"*Weren't* we? Going to be a *lovely* spring day!"

Over by the pond there's a little crowd of people, medieval and modern, around two knights having a slow-motion battle with huge swords. The blades clang and the shields clash, but it all looks pretty light-hearted and harmless—the guys are laughing at each other's jokes as they swing away.

I walk towards them uncertainly. My guy at home—this might be the costume party he belongs to. I should tell someone here about him. Relief washes through me; I can hand him over to someone else? But when I get to the fight I walk slowly around the outside of the circle. Those medieval-dressed people, they look so *clean* . . . and those veils flying from the ladies' pointed hats would *have* to be synthetic . . . I try to spot someone who might be in charge, some bustling innkeeper, some queen or baron. Maybe one of the fighters is the person I should inform? I fold my arms and stand there unde-cided.

Then the sword-fighters clinch, the two blades pointing straight up between them. And beyond the blades, swinging in at the park gate and striding straight towards us, is the guy from the beach.

There's no mistaking him, even though he's wearing a helmet now, and a monster sword slung across his back—it's his size that tells me, his rock-chunky build, the sick feeling in my stomach.

Stillness falls around him as he crosses the park, as if he's scything the life out of everyone he passes. When he gets to us, the crowd falls still, too, and then the knights notice, and stop fighting. People's jaws drop; they glance at each other, and then back, expectantly, at this . . . this . . .

You know how people say, "She brought a breath of fresh air into the room"? Well, this warrior, he brings with him not a breath but a *gust*, not fresh but *strange* air. I don't know how to describe it, but very suddenly I know a few things about him: that he's come for *me*, for a start. He's not one of these dress-up-and-play knights; this is not his party—he's not from anything as frivolous as a party (what was I thinking?). He's from somewhere else in a serious way, from somewhere beyond anywhere I know, from some complete *other*-where.

I mean, he is *foreign*. He's some different species of human from what I'm used to. The armour—I've handled it, I've seen it up close—it's got a different history, it's made with a whole different *technology* from the armour these knights are wearing. The guy's muscles have built up out of different movements than we make in daily life. The eyes, hidden now behind a chain-mail veil across the front of the helmet, they come from seeing some place, some life—some reality—so utterly different from Sunny Bay, or from the city—

This is all coming to me in a single gasp of thought. Then the guy calls out to me across the circle, something calm and matter-of-fact, like, *We had an arrangement, remember. We'll go home now.* Oh, you can *hear* the strangeness, the words almost all consonants, not squishing and buzzing like Russian or clicking like those little Kalahari guys, but doing absolutely its own thing, making its own kind of sense.

I pick up my shopping and push forward through the crowd. "'Scuse me. I know this guy," I say into the silence, and suddenly everyone's slack-jawed attention is on me, too. "Thanks. Excuse me."

He escorts me from the park.

"Hey, where'd he get those pants made?" one of the knights calls out as we go.

"Shut up, Trev," says the other.

We get off the main street, away from the Saturday morning traffic. Beside me the chain-mail pants make a soft *sloosh* with every step. I'm trying to see how his wound is, but the strap of the sword-sheath covers that part of his side, so that I can't see either the wound or a bandage of any kind. No fresh blood on his trousers, no inflammation on the visible skin. And the injury isn't bothering him at all. I can hardly believe this is the same guy who nearly collapsed on me a few hours ago.

"Your side," I say. "How is it?" He keeps walking. I touch his arm and point to *my* side, then his. He hooks the strap away from his body so I can see the dark welt where the bullet hole was.

"Wha-at? But how'd you do that?" There's no blood, no scab, no torn flesh, just a layer of pearly new skin sealing over the wound.

He's wearing a gap-toothed grin, his eyes no more than gleams behind the helmet mail. Hmm, a fully operational foreign warrior, that's quite a different thing from an incapacitated one. Why's he *looking* at me like that? What's he planning?

When we get home I really worry. The screen door, which I locked on the way out, is kicked off its hinges and bent almost in half, still attached by the lock on the other side. "Oh, what?" I moan. "Did you do that?"

But he's gone on past the house, stepping over the back gate and heading off into the dunes. "Oh. Well, thanks a *lot*. For all your *help*, Mr. Self-Healing, Self-Bloody-Contained—"

I bang my way inside, glad he's out of the way.

I get started on the soup. Sizzled onion and bacon smells start warming the house. When everything's chopped and thrown into the stock, I'm ready to tackle Marnie's room. I zip off the mattress cover and put it in the washing machine with all the other bloody cloth. I spend a long clumsy time on the porch pouring water into the foam mattress and stamping it out again until it runs clear. I wash down all the bloodied surfaces and sweep up the sand, hang out the washing. I rinse all the armour plate and the arrow-bullet and put them on the ugly little Formica coffee table in the living room.

At that point the warrior bursts in. The front door-handle crashes into the wall; a fresh load of sand drops in chunks from his boots. He seizes the bread that's on the kitchen counter, tears off half of it and goes out again, without so much as grunting at me.

I stand there looking at the sandy floor, at the mangled bread. The soup lid *glunk*s gently on the pot. It's quiet except for the birds, and the distant breathing of the sea, and my own breathing. I'm really tired, I realise—and not just from getting up before dawn. I'm deeply, long-term tired, emptied out, sick of cleaning up other people's messes, sick of *being* James's resident mess, sick of try-try-trying and always failing, always having someone—if not James, then Conan the Barbarian here or *someone*—barge in and trample all over what I've done. I won't tidy any more, I decide; I'll just wait and see what happens, and tidy up at the end—*maybe*. If I *feel* like it.

I fetch a couple of blankets from Marnie's room and lie down on the couch where I can see the door. No sirens, no traffic sounds, no possibility of a phone ring-ing—only birds, breeze, soup pot, sea, and me.

| | | |

The finned bullet is the first thing I see when I wake up. I reach out of my blanket-cocoon and pick it up. It's heavy. It all but fills my hand. And it's sharp; it gives me a low, sick feeling to think of it *choonk*ing into a person, sitting second-knuckle-deep inside a live body, fizzing out its poison. But it did choonk, it did sit. It's all really happening.

I get up and ladle myself out some soup. It's dim in here, at five o'clock. I turn on the lights and close the curtains against the darkening bush-scape. Sit down, eat. Everything's so quiet. *Maybe he won't come back,* I think hopefully.

I'm halfway through my soup when I hear a *sloosh* outside, a thump of boots on the patio. *Rattle-rattle* of the doorhandle. *Crash* against the wall. I cringe low, my face practically in my bowl.

"Aaah!" He grins at me—Christ, what a wreck of a face! Then he goes to the soup pot and fills his mouth direct from the ladle.

I jump up. "Hey, don't be a *pig*! Here, sit down, at least." I grab the ladle from him and push him towards the table. Suddenly everything in the house seems small and dinky, the Sixties chairs, the bowls. The spoons look like fairy spoons!

In the end I put the pot in front of him and give him a big old battered silver serving spoon. He eats soup until there's no more soup, bread until there's no more bread. He eats like a person who doesn't know about tables and cutlery, crouched over the bowl slurping. I watch him as I finish my own soup, worrying, *How long is he planning to stay? I don't know if I can keep the fuel up to this person. Not to mention, what does a guy like this do after dinner?*

He gets up, wiping his mouth on his hand. He goes to

the coffee table and picks up his washed shirt, eyeing it from all sides before putting it on. Immediately he looks a bit more domesticated. Then the mail-shirt, then the leather shirt. He ties on all the plate armour he can, but brings the tail-pieces across to me, turns his back and waves a hand where they should go. "O-kay. This I can do." So long as clothes keep going *on* rather than coming *off* . . .

When his back's re-plated, he goes to the door. He jerks his head at me, *Come on*, and goes out. I pull on my boots, grab my jumper and the torch and follow him, shutting and locking the door behind me, just in case this takes a while.

He's standing at the back gate. When he sees me coming he disappears into the dunes. I follow him down to the beach and shine the torch around.

"Hey, you've been busy here." He's dragged together a huge pile of driftwood, propping it against the giant dead tree trunk that several summers' worth of our family bonfires haven't managed to burn away.

He takes the torch from me and holds it to a nest of dry seaweed and paper litter in the side of the pile. He's surprised when it doesn't catch alight; he touches the torch-end tentatively and then in scorn and amazement, and tosses it towards me. He gets a flint and steel from a pouch tucked in at the top of his pants, and lights the fire that way, using fine frazzled seaweed to catch the sparks. Very delicate work for such big hands.

He builds it up bigger than any bonfire I've ever seen, a huge orange flag flapping against the stars. The heat pushes me gradually back up the beach to the edge of the dunes. The warrior strides about wielding a big long branch to stir up the flames; all the while he's singing, some tuneless, growling, energetic song, but only snatches of it reach me through the fire-roar.

And then other people start turning up, stepping into the firelight and bellowing greetings, *rough* people, others of his kind. They're a cross between a biker gang and a bunch of bag-people, all leather and dirt. The women are strong and snaggle-toothed, and several go bare-breasted. Some are pregnant, their bellies armoured like silvery armadillo-backs. The men are all built like brick outhouses, with shaved heads or messy, long hair like my guy's. Men, women, and children, they're all scarred somehow, all tattooed somewhere, and all wear some kind of armour, sometimes just the plate, sometimes just the mail, sometimes the whole kit right down to the finger-guards.

They bring stuff. They bring this dark-red drink, with a head on it like beer, and big metal cups to drink it from. They bring bread that's almost black, with what look like small yellow chunks of stone all through it. And they bring—I don't know how, I can't *think* from where—a gigantic black-bristled dead pig, with tusks, hanging from a pole, and they dig a pit with their bare hands, and they line it with hot coals and hot stones, and bury the pig to cook it. I guess we're in for a long night.

A girl with good teeth approaches me—the first, it seems, to notice me—and with lots of bowing and hand signs gives me a mug of the red drink. She sits down next to me, drinking her own drink and talking nonstop between gulps. I'm not a big drinker, so I just sip at first. It tastes kind of fine and foul at the same time—a touch of sweetness and a lot of sourness and a chili-heat that blanks out all the taste after the first few sips.

As for what it does to my brain . . . After half a mug I

feel as if someone's gone over the inside of my skull with a pot scourer, and is rinsing it out with hot water. I put the mug down firmly in the sand beside me. I feel intensely physically well coordinated all of a sudden, and as if—ah! at last!—I'm starting to see life clearly. It's really very simple, when you think about it properly. If only this girl would stop gabbing at me, I'd be able to concentrate and sort out every single thing that's bothering me. I'd get it straight in my own brain, in my own way of saying things; I'd go back to James, and I'd say, so confidently—

But she keeps on. And then—it's not quite as good as those dreams where you pick up a flute and start blowing beautiful music out of it, but I find I can tell her sentences apart, and in each sentence there's a key word that sense comes out of, sometimes combined with a gesture—throwing the spear, cutting the beast's throat, driving a stake into the ground. And I forget about James-and-what-I-should-say-to-convince-him, and focus instead on grasping the meaning in her talk. It's not easy, but it's fascinating. I can feel myself becoming a different person as I listen; a whole world is opening up inside my head, this girl's world, the warrior's world, that other-where world.

And then the bandits were on us, she says. *Only a little group, but they had good weapons, must have traded them all down the country from Rivermouth. Kun-asta went down and Lie-Bold, our best, and then—I guess our fear was great enough to thin the world-skin.*

"Huh?" I don't quite trust my ears on that last bit.

She laughs, the drink red on her teeth. *Oh, I know, your call did the main work. But a saint's need must meet an equal need, to breach the skins of worlds.*

My "call"? A "saint"? They're hard words to get my

mouth around in her language. *You mean me?*

This is a saint-realm; you must be the saint, she says matter-of-factly, and takes another swig. *Oh, good, they're making a fight-circle. Come down and watch.*

Down on the harder sand, we help dig out a hand-deep gutter around an area the size of a sumo-wrestling ring. Then the duels start. There's wrestling and there's fighting with sticks and swords. The toddlers go first, these little feral kids stumbling after each other in the sand; everybody loves that. Then it's older girls and boys, carefully matched, and the rules are clearer: you start and finish with an embrace; you pull your punches when your opponent's really at a disadvantage—you show that you *could* hammer someone, you don't actually do it—

Whenever I drain my mug, someone comes around with a big brown skin flask and refills it. There's boisterous singing going on behind me, fast and complicated with outbreaks of laughter—if I could take my eyes off the fighting I'd love to turn around and concentrate on that for a while. But as the pairs and groups of fighters get older and better, I start to feel uneasy: surely they won't expect *me* . . . ?

Teeth-girl gets up, slapping my shoulder. She calls out for a shirt for me. Oh, my *God*, here we go, into major embarrassment. I take a big swig of the drink and stand up.

I get a mail-shirt—it's heavy—and a sword that I do have some hope of hefting. I follow the girl onto the fighting-ground. Huge, bright-eyed, filthy people are all around, all of them, down to the toddlers, better fighters than me.

But I'm learning—I'm quickly hugged and then I'm learning. At first she's doing all the moving, using the tip of her sword to show me how I should respond. As soon as

I start to make my own plays, shouts go up all around, and she grins, and makes an obvious, foolish error that leaves her bare side exposed. I'm in there, my blade poking at her ribs, straight away—she laughs, and spreads her arms, presenting me to the others—some of the little kids look a bit pitying, but all the older people laugh and call out approval.

We go a couple more rounds, one in which she pins me, the last she lets me win. Then she sheaths her sword and hugs me. *Plenty to learn, but plenty learnt,* is the gist of what she says into my ear.

We walk out of the circle. My bruises are throbbing; my hands can still feel the handle, my arms the weight, of the sword; I'm tingling all over with the heat of my own movement, sweating in the fire's glow, sand in my hair from being knocked to the ground.

Now I'm ready to get into the singing. But something makes me look up—a firelit figure on the dunes, tall, slender as a greyhound, staring down at all this in utter disbelief. James.

Run up there. Tell him. Explain, say my instincts. Feelings—relief, joy, love—swoop through me, a familiar fly-past. But instead of flying with them up the dune, I stand, weighed down by the mail-shirt and the sword. I see the shadowy banners those shiny little aeroplanes drag after them, the other feelings: my fear of James's opinion, the pain of holding myself in this unnatural shape he professes to love, the anger at all the crap I take, all the ground I give, because I think that's love, I think that's a marriage—or *thought* it until, now, there's nothing left of me, and James is married to a shadow-James, with all the life and interest and *self* squashed out of her.

I can't go up to him. I can't apologise again. I can't be

embarrassed for myself, or for these wild people around me. There is no explanation, only the flash of their eyes in the firelight, only the *sloosh* of my mail-shirt as I lift my arm.

"Come down, James!" I call out.

Of course he doesn't; he won't ever. He thinks he'd be sullying himself. He wants me to go up there, so he can *tell* me stuff: that *he's* decided to give us another chance. But actually, he's having doubts now—who are these people? Look, his hands are on his hips. What right have I got to come down to Sunny Bay and *party*? I'm supposed to be prostrate, weeping, curled around my mobile in the foetal position. *But I haven't rung you all night and all day, have I, James? Better ring up Marnie, find out where I am, start reeling me in by the umbilical cord—again.*

Well, I don't think so.

The singers stop, glancing from James to me. Some of them crawl to either side, so that there's a pathway through to the dune.

"No," I say in their language. "I'm not going. Not this time."

Scowling, James takes a couple of steps down the dune. I draw a deep breath. I breathe in and in and in, as if my whole body is one great big lung. More people crawl out of the way. I open my mouth, meaning to shout *No! Go away!*, good and loud and final.

What comes out of me is fire. A roar of fire, a blast of fire, a curling, teeming, many-coloured chameleon-tongue of fire. It curves up the dune-side and scorches the scrub at the top. James's spread hand, with the wedding ring on it, sticks out like a drowning man's. He falls, he claws himself upright, he flounders flaming up over the dune-top and out of sight. He may be screaming—I hear nothing. The pain of breathing fire from my whole body has picked me up, flipped me back and forth like a dying fish, and dropped me, white-hot and without breath, onto the sand.

| | | |

Att-sada wakes me with a tiny shake, her fingers pinching my lips closed. The rain has eased; the dune-grass is all furry silver with rain-drops and fog-drops. All around me the people rise from sleep with slow care, hushing the children; the beasts in this country are too big for us, and we must move through without them catching our scent or sound. We're on our way to the spring country, where there'll be fruit and grains to eat as well as beast, and fewer bandits to plague us. We'll follow the coast a long and lonely way, then cut inland at the tip of the mountain range.

Kun-asta comes towards us, waking people, greeting with a look or touch. Oh, God—I try to look invisible.

Last night he and Lie-Bold were the final pair in the fight-circle, when the singing had stopped and the children were asleep. I watched him and I was mortified for ever thinking he was rough or ugly or smelly. I've never seen anything as beautiful as his duel with Lie-Bold, the speed and strength of it. It was like watching the workings of a smart, complicated machine, a machine for weaving, for loosening and re-locking, for combining thousands of smooth, high-polished movements in new ways. They fought on and on, and I sat dazed and dazzled by the leap and brace, the topple and save and search of the fighting. And at the end, when Lie-Bold conceded and Kun-asta stood laughing in his embrace, holding his injured side, the two of them panting almost too hard to laugh, I put down my head and gave in to my illness and upheaval, and sobs caught me by the throat and shook me. Att-sada and the others laid their hard hands on my head and shoulders. *So much to learn,* was all I could get out. *So far to go.*

Kun-asta turns to Att-sada and me. *Can you travel, Billie-saint?* he says, very quietly. *Can you walk?*

I raise my gaze from his worn boots to his sore-looking red eyes. There's still some infection in him, from the bandits' missile, just as there's leftover burning all through me. For a moment my sympathy overrides my awe and I can sort of smile; for a tiny second his awesomeness wavers and he might be a young man again, maybe as young as me.

My gaze sinks to his boots again. *I can walk,* I say, feeling lighter and frailer than a floating leaf of ash. *I may fight like a blind bear, but I can put one foot in front of the other.*

A quiet ripple of laughter spreads out from us. *Blind bear—What did the saint say?—Said she fights like a—*

But Kun-asta doesn't smile. *Let's do it, then,* he says, *Let's put one foot in front of the other.*

And he moves on, and so do we all move on; all together, we walk out of the dunes onto the beach. We head northward along the hard sand, while the fog slowly tumbles ashore, by turns thinning to show us the headland and thickening to blot it from our sight.

| | | |

THE

NIGHT

LILY

When Dulcet died, Marda stopped telling stories—to Parda, to Chenko and of course to Dulcet, who'd pretended to be too old but always hung by, listening by mistake. "Story's all gone to hell in a paper boat," Marda had wept, "when a child can be picked out of his life, without hardly beginning it."

| | | |

He called it the Lily. It wasn't white. It wasn't a girl. But the Lily was its name the minute he saw it.

It wasn't a beautiful thing. Chenko had seen plenty of innards in his short time and this, in short, was innards. It piled and looped and swung like innards; it was mauves and pale greens and white-veiled pinks like innards; it glistened like innards. But it didn't act like innards, and it didn't have innards' offal breath. It smelt the way water used to taste, of a blue lake among pine trees.

Of a night-time, it came out to hang, heavily, above Chenko and his bedding. It lived in the head-space of the wardrobe, where the house-canker had grown so bad that anything stored there would stink of rotten concrete forever after. (But the Lily never stank.) Maybe it had followed him knowing he had room for it, seeing he was perhaps the one kid in this city who did.

| | | |

When the Duwazza picked Dulcet off, there was no family or friend left to put in that room with Chenko.

"Don't tell anyone we have a space," said Marda tiredly. "I don't want to take anyone in, or anyone's anyone. You got me?"

Chenko nodded. He wasn't likely to tell, didn't she know? Dulcet was the one who did the talking, made the friends. And the girlfriends—did Marda know about that? Nifty Imogen Dawsey with her two amazing golden plaits, who'd been smithereened with her brother in the underground cinema a week before Dulcet got his. Smithereened or cindered—sometimes it was hard to tell which.

| | | |

It followed him home. What else could he do but take it in?

"'way you, Chenko Zlatter!" the really-big boys had been calling down the street. And he had been 'waying, good and quiet. A stone or something had just popped him in the ankle, making his heart skip, but he'd been moving on, no worries.

He'd gone past Dugget Cave, the big hole where Annerley Dugget and his four girls got theirs. It was just slightly bigger than a lot of caves along there. When he thought back later, the Lily must've come out of Dugget's. It must have been hiding where there was just that bit more space; it knew that kind of place, it scouted out that kind of place.

There was a hum about it that was nearly a tune, nearly not a sound at all, but he felt it, that first time. There was no one else on the street by then—only, behind and a bit above him, this trailing, almost-singing thing, the Lily.

| | | |

It wasn't as if the Duwazza needed Dulcet. There were plenty of street-dwellers for their pleasure. Like everyone, Chenko hurried daily past those terrible silences with their bellies zlitted open and spilling on the street. There'd been that bad day with the

heads spiked all along the park fence—some brave person had
cleared that the next night. And all the time he was stepping over
the general litter of pieces that lay for no more than a day, winter
or summer, in winter white like pieces of statue, in summer black
with flies.

| | | |

That day had been a latchkey day. They lived in one of a
few blocks that had doors—and mostly unbroken windows, except on the south side from the June blasts—so
there actually were latches, that worked. He opened the
door and the Lily sidled in after him. When he'd snicked
all the locks and slid all the chains across, he turned and it
was there, rearranging itself in the air so that he got
glimpses of its shiny, crimson, slightly ruffled inner
organs.

He offered the Lily food, which it politely declined.
He poured some water into the bowl they had, and it lowered a part of itself, pale blue-mauve and like a long thin
toadstool, and took up half the water like that. He walked
back and forth a lot between the kitchen and his bedroom, softly past sleeping Parda's door, for the fascination
of having it come after him. He lay on his bedding and it
stretched out above him in all its glistening loops and
clumps, and hummed, and shifted companionably.
Chenko thought, *This is what pet dogs must have been like.*
Except dogs didn't hum—at least, not in stories.

| | | |

The Duwazza had dogs, to bring in the game. Two of them
would have clamped onto Dulcet's shoulders and dragged him

back to the van from where he'd been picked off. He might easily have still been alive then, feeling the teeth, hearing the panting in both ears. Chenko couldn't think about that for long.

(Where had the hole been? Where had the blood been running from? Or had he been zlitted, with more than blood dragging out behind? It bothered him not to know, but it would bother Marda worse to be asked.)

| | | |

Next day he rushed home, frightened the Lily had run away—or worse, never been there at all. He swung into his room and his heart crashed and he flung himself on the bedding, already at work: *You can manage. It doesn't matter.*

And the wardrobe-cloth twitched aside, and the Lily came out, and its hum started, like Dulcet's valve radio warming up.

"Oh, you *are* here," Chenko said, smiling up at it.

But the Lily didn't answer anything, by sound or by movement, ever.

| | | |

Marda hugged him. "Ah, you smell like *something*, Chenk!" She drew in a long breath of him. "You find some soap?"

Chenko shook his head.

She punched his shoulder. "Been sitting next to some sweet-flavoured *girl?*"

"Nope, no way."

"You sure now?"

He was too pleased to hear her teasing and see her

smiling to bother being embarrassed. "I'm sure. What would I need a *girl* for?"

She laughed outright. Then, "Oh," she said wistfully, "a girl can be nice." And he remembered that she was one, and he didn't know how to say sorry, so he draped himself on her again, and that seemed to work just as well.

| | | | |

The war would leave you alone for as long as you didn't want anything too badly. Chenko was surprised Dulcet hadn't seen that. He could've told him: the moment you fixed on that girl, you might as well have shelled her yourself.

And then Chenko's own worry had helped bring it on—first, his wondering, Should I warn Dulcet?, then, when he heard about the cinema, Dulcet will take this so badly; he's the one in danger now. Chenko had tried to stay calm, to banish the worry as soon as it came to him, but still Dulcet had got it, on the very way home from the cinema people's funeral. Chenko was startled—he thought he'd have more time than that, he thought Dulcet'd have more time—but if he thought about it, it made sense, the way the war always went.

| | | | |

Nights, the Lily was there like a lamp, beaming something, but not light. With every flash outside, it was in a different place, piled in the damp-stain corner, puddling right above him with all its undersides flat on some air layer, hanging all baggy at the window. One night he woke and it was spread around the moonlit room like oil dribbled on water; its bare organs leaned in a clump near the door, swaying very gently. He reached up, touching nothing, just to feel the humming, like a soft bangle on his wrist. Over in the darkest corner some part of the Lily coiled and settled, as if it had noticed.

Even the big blasts did no more than send a tremor through it. On bad nights when Chenko lay stiff as a corpse in his bed, scared almost to move his eyes, still the Lily only hovered, making its same slow turnings from place to place.

| | | |

He took thin-soup into Marda and Parda's fusty room, that was full of Parda's illness.

"Who opened the window?" His old man was getting whiter by the day, slowly all of him going the colour of his hair. "Who let the sunshine in?"

"It's Chenko."

"Chenko, son! You are a sight for sore noses. You are a field fulla spring flowers." Parda hadn't made sense in a long time.

Chenko smiled. "I've got some soup for you here, Par."

"Blessed boy." Parda looked up out of his whitening eyes. "Blessed boy."

| | | |

It was very cold in Miz Izbister's bedroom. Some of the kids had brought blankets, some were using Miz Izbister's. Chenko had come too late for even a corner of one.

Bang, thud. Miz Izbister quickly set up the old play-blackboard. She was nervous with the activity outside, Duwazza hollers and the odd shot.

Maylette came in late, dressed thinly. She picked a way in among the kids on the floor, right back to Chenko against the wall. Since Dulcet got his there'd been a space next to him on Miz Izbister's yellow-rosed grey carpet. Maylette slipped in there and took some shuddering breaths.

"Today is the life cycle of the duck," said Miz Izbister.

Maylette gasped from the cold and her teeth rattled. She smiled a tight, apologetic smile at Chenko.

He put his feet apart and beckoned her. She scrambled crabwise in to him. The cold of her spindly back sucked the heat out of his belly; her arms and her legs were like slim cold-iron poles against his. The shivers went through her, and through again, but got slower bit by bit, and round about the time the duck and the curly-tail drake were getting together, she started making her own warmth, and giving some of Chenko's back.

| | | |

Parda went quietly, in a quiet night. Chenko had put two spoonfuls of broth into him the evening before, wiped Parda's mouth and made way for Marda to do the bathroom stuff.

Marda hadn't come into Chenko's room for a long time. It had been Dulcet's room, too, and Dulcet's stuff was still around—the dead radio, a little tossed clothing. As Chenko woke, he was already checking behind Marda as she bent, but there was only a twitchlet of movement in the wardrobe-cloth, and no hum.

Marda was using a strange voice, deep and very frightened. "It's only you and me now, Chenko. What a world to be left in."

She had already washed Parda, and he lay neat, his top half dressed in the beautiful shirt for going to the funeral parlour, the rest of him covered with the throw rug because there were no trousers or shoes that went with the shirt. Or there were, but they'd been on Dulcet, and you don't get those things back from the Duwazza. You don't get anything back—except the head, if they know you and hate you.

Parda wasn't so different from his sleeping self—and yet he was, *so* different, so gone from behind that candle-lit face. Chenko's chest ached, hearing Parda's voice clearly, knowing the voice would get quieter and go, with his old man gone.

He leaned against Marda as she wept, then as she gradually slept. Just when he was dozing himself, the Lily came out of his room; he heard it investigating the hallway. It eased in and lay above Parda awhile, like a many-coloured cloud. All the rest of the night it sailed slowly from room to room, spreading out long and tumbling back together, trying new resting places, gently stirring all the apartment's air.

| | | |

Miz Izbister at last got together a battery and showed them a few minutes of her lover-lamp. But the globs were only red, and just globbed up and down. Chenko sat quiet up the back, marvelling—the Lily was so, *so* much better! Every shape it made was different, and every part of it had different colour, vein work, muscle movement, scallop and frill.

"It's very calming," Miz Izbister said after a moment of silence when she'd explained the workings.

"Mmm," said Maylette among others, but Maylette was leaning out of her corner to see around Annibell's head, and her chopped black hair was flopping onto Chenko's shoulder.

Maylette was smart, too smart for most boys. She wasn't mean or ugly, but she had a frightening brain that she sometimes let out on a long leash. But if he could guarantee she wouldn't tell anyone else, or speak there in the room with the Lily, he might show Maylette. She might be the one he could show.

Miz Izbister held him back after class. "I heard about your parda."

Chenko nodded stiffly.

"It's been a hard few months for you Zlatters."

"Oh, not as hard as some people's." It was what Marda might say.

She sighed and sagged, and put her hands on his shoulders and squeezed. "No one would mind if you cried."

He looked up, surprised. Crying? He hadn't cried since—oh, way back. Even during the June blasts—just shaking, that time, just lying wide-eyed, curled up and shaking. He remembered, laughing a little, a time when he'd cried several times every day, mostly to get Dulcet into trouble.

"No, it's okay," he said to Miz Izbister.

She smiled in a way that didn't get to her eyes. "I know you'll look after your mother, and she after you."

Put like that, it did sound like something to cry over.

He nodded again, not wanting to look impatient, and she let go.

"If you need anything . . ."

"Thank you, I will."

And he was out in the corridor, climbing over the rubble towards the lobby.

| | | |

Maylette came to the funeral parlour with Parda's few friends that were left. She brought a jar of peanut butter.

Marda gasped when she saw it. "Where'd you get that, lovely-girl?"

"Sh," said Maylette. "We have a little stash."

"So kind!" Marda hid it in her bag straight away.

While the grown-ups talked, Chenko and Maylette went out onto the porch, because there was weak sunlight there, and morning was a safer time. They shoved their hands in their pockets and looked out over the craters. A lot of firepower had been spent on this park, where there'd been no buildings to flatten, only trees. Chenko raised his eyes to the gap between the distant church spire and the wrecked TV tower—somewhere in there was their apartment.

| | | |

Chenko had walked all the way here when he'd heard about the trees, but of course every carry-able piece down to kindling scraps had been taken by the time he got here. There was a woman with a chainsaw, and two big daughters and an old man with a stick to guard the petrol and the cut wood. The way they looked at Chenko, he said nothing; he turned around, and walked home.

| | | |

"That jar," said Chenko.

Maylette smiled. "A swipe. Pantry in Northside Park." She was wearing a hibiscus-splashed shirt, huge, the sleeves rolled thickly at her elbows; eight-inch cuffs were folded up on her overall legs. Dressed up special, with her hair washed and combed. It gave Chenko a strange feeling, a hovering somewhere deep, between his navel and his groin.

"You must be good."

Her smile went further, and he laughed. Then the call-bell sounded inside, and he felt all the expression go from his face. Down in a crater in the park a loose length of UXB tape was fluttering, faded to palest pink.

For a quick shock of a moment, Maylette was right against him, her thin arms holding him, her clean cotton hibiscus-sleeve under his nose. Then she stepped back, frowning, and drew him around to face the parlour door. Inside, a huffy pedal-organ began to play.

| | | |

No one believes these songs, Marda had said. We wish we did, but we don't—not a word. But we still use them. What else would we use?

In the middle of the ragged final chorus came the whistle-*crump*, whistle-*crump* of distant shelling. The singing tailed off and people looked up and around as they always did, as if things in this room would clue them to any danger.

Then the acting priest-man went over and closed Parda away behind the curtains. Next to Chenko, Marda pulled in a very deep and unsteady breath and straightened. On his other side Maylette snatched her hands off the prayer-rail and tucked them into her armpits.

"Oh, my," said Marda on the porch. Smoke was going up, a wall of smoke from the dead TV tower as far as the bridge. You couldn't see the church for smoke. "Oh my, oh my. Oh, Par." And she had to sit down.

"I'll go," said Chenko. "You stay here. Or go to . . . Mrs Abel, can she come to you?"

"I've got her. Don't worry. I even have tea."

Maylette ran with him. There was a lot of rubble between them and home, a lot of scrambling. They got into the smoke and the wailing, and it was hard to tell where they were with all the new caves and fallen walls. But Chenko kept a handle on things—the keystone of the church archway, the green GET HOME ALIVE posters on the school's only wall, an actual street-sign, Bay Street and Hoe, intact even to its useless lamp.

They found the *place*, at least. They found the smithereens. Some dead were already brought out and laid in a row. A province-woman was sobbing there over her half a daughter.

"It's a good thing it's morning," said Maylette. "You'll have time to find a cave."

They paced out the hall, worked out where the Zlatters' rubble was, started tossing bricks aside, chunks of cankered concrete. It always amazed Chenko how much *more* there was of a house, knocked down.

All they found was Dulcet's old satchel, the kitchen pot, some bedding. Chenko hauled the wardrobe-cloth out too, scattering bricks. He felt all over its yellow and brown daisies. It wasn't wet, or dirty with anything other than brick-filth.

He couldn't be surprised. Things disappeared under shells. Shells blew brick to powder, flesh to spray. And the Lily had been, if anything, soft.

Still, he sat down. The province-woman's noise was clambering around in his head. And it was sunny, and as safe as it ever would be.

Maylette crossed the sliding rubble and sat down, too. She waved the squashed stove in front of his wet eyes. "One thing you don't have to hope for," she said, and tossed it away. Her other arm was on his back, right where the sweat was coldest.

"It's just, *Dulcet* and then *Parda* and then—" He folded the wardrobe-cloth. "It was a good place!" he burst out, and was properly crying. "Doors—you could lock—my parda could be sick there—"

"Yep." She rubbed his back, hurting. It helped.

And she left her arm on him. It was so luxurious, there in the sun, that he stole some unrelated crying—just a small burst, quickly curbed.

"Nothing fair about it," said Maylette in a finishing way, as he slowed.

He nodded, mopped up on his sleeve. Maylette wore a mask of dust; sweat stripes ran from her temples to her chin. She'd tied her shirt around her middle. "You dirtied up your nice clothes," he said.

She looked at herself, grinned, shrugged. "We done here?"

"I think so."

He picked up the bundle of bedding and followed her off the rubble. She stood right by him as he looked back, her gritty arm against his. He could still *tell* her about the Lily.

But right now, Marda needed to know what was left.

The smoke was clearing; the dead were covered with plastic sheeting; the province-woman was gone. As Maylette and Chenko worked their way out, cries from the market—*Candles! Potatoes! A green bean for a gold tooth!*—echoed as usual from street to street.

THE BOY

WHO   T

N

I should have realised straight off. Of all people, I, Tess Maxwell, should've seen him for what he was. I mean, I knew something was different, something big. My eyes kept going back to him. But I was caught up in people leaving the Art Cottage, and he was in the crowd going to the basketball courts, and we got swept away from each other, Keenoy Ribson and me.

I tried to work it out at the bus stop, the way you try and get a whole dream back using the one little shred you remember. But it turned into a flutter among flutters in my mind, and the bus came, and I went home.

I went home and I went to work—same place. I work in one square of home; "the parlour," Mum calls it, a polite name for such a messy, personal kind of business premises.

My first client was a woman who was after her husband. He was right there with her, of course; the thick, dark string of his tether went from his worn slipper-toe to her right shoulder. He hung over her, griping.

"He's saying 'Don't burn the snags, Merrill,'" I told her.

She laughed. "Oh yes, of course. Yes, that's him. Same old whingeing bludger. God, I miss him!" And she cried. They always cry when you tell them that kind of detail.

And then there was a man. He had a very handsome boyfriend—well, the handsome version alternated with a blotched, dying one who slid down to lie between us on the Turkish rug. "He's very grateful for everything you did for him," I said. "It made it easier, he says. You did everything right. Robert, his name is." And the guy nodded, and he dissolved in tears, too. "You're doing good work," I went on. "You think it's pointless without Robert, but every day of your life you make a big difference to a lot of people. He's not saying that; it's just . . . clear, around you. There's all this value; you're very solid. What *is* your work?"

"I'm a nurse," he said, through the complimentary tissues.

"Oh, there you go, then."

After him, I was tired, because it *is* tiring. But two clients means a hundred dollars. Five hundred dollars a week is a good amount—it means we can live, as well as keep Dad at Bernard House. If I were *really determined* I could do more, but . . . but I guess I'm not. We're managing, aren't we? We're managing fine on two a night.

Mum was in the kitchen with a fruit-shake and a cheese muffin for me, and Dad was there, too, on homecare. I sat and ate and thought about bed.

"Take Dad for a walk?" said Mum.

I nodded. It was too early for bed; a walk would clear my head ready for homework.

It was cold outside, grey and darkening. I wheeled Dad up to the park, because the paths there have got nice, rounded corners, and I needed to be somewhere quiet, among trees and rotundas and curly metal seats. I started to wake up there, I started to come back to myself. You can't hurry that; all you can do is wait.

| | | |

I used to exhaust myself over Dad. It didn't do any good. I can feel his brain almost as if it's in my own skull, and half of it's just drained, of juice, of life. And nothing on the living side's very strong, either. Everything shimmers at the same level, with no memory bigger or better than the others, and there are no links between the memories, or feelings tied to them; everything's just random poppings-up, a sort of play of life like a small, settled fire that won't actually burn anything up.

Once, right back at the beginning, Mum asked what I could see. "They say the life force can flow back in, bit by bit," she said. And she looked up from Dad, wanting hope—from *me*, probably the only person in her world who couldn't give her any.

I was so embarrassed for her I couldn't speak. *Life force*—where'd she get that idea? And who were "they" supposed to be?

"But that'd be for *mild* strokes, I suppose," she finished, turning away.

I recovered a bit. "He's there, but he's all mulched up. He doesn't hang together."

"Is there any point," she asked, "in it being us, who look after him? Does it make any difference? Does he recognise us?"

"Not very often. And not much happens when he does."

Which was why we eventually put him in Bernard House, to get some life back for ourselves, some time *not* tending that fire. We do still tend it, but only on a few weeknights. Mum wheels Dad home and parks him in the kitchen–family room he designed and built, and feeds him while I work—she says she doesn't want me feeding him, doesn't want me to have memories of that. And she talks to him. She's hoping to get something back, an eye-flicker, a noise that sounds like an answer. Stubbornly she goes on, serenely talking, about the news, about people they both used to know (but now only she knows them), goes on and on breaking her heart over him—or maybe not breaking it so much as wearing it away, grinding it gradually down to nothing.

I won't do that to myself. I know it upsets Mum that I don't talk to Dad, but what's the point if he doesn't exist enough to hear me? Mum still thinks he does—time and time again I see her making up that alternative life, seeing his eyes brighten, watching him throw off his rug and stand up: *I'll just get that doorknob fixed before dinner,* he says, or *What are we all sitting around here for, with long faces?* But even when his voice is so clear, coming through her, I can't believe; I *know* Dad's kind of damage never mends. He won't come back.

| | | |

Next morning I woke up breathing the deep calm of a Dad-free house. *Whatsaname Ribson,* I thought. *Keenoy. The air around him is absolutely clear and silent.* Yeah, that was it. No strings attached him to any yearnings or losses. He was clean; he was himself; he was completely self-contained. Like me. Excitement stirred tentatively under my ribs. *Could* there be someone like that? Or did he have some attachment I just wasn't seeing yet?

I dressed and took coffee in to Mum, stroked her head to wake her up and gave her one of those big morning hugs—better than coffee, she says—which are like being drunk out of, but like drinking, too. And I smiled back at her, which I can do, some mornings.

"Busy day ahead?" she said. Beside her the bedclothes were flat and uncluttered, where for a long time after Dad's stroke there'd been a mound, a Dad-shaped mound that Mum had put there.

"Busy day every day. Want toast?"

"There are some muffins left—I'll have one of those. Please, I mean."

"Your wish is my command."

"Thanks, love."

| | | |

Going up the hill to school, I saw a tall boy's curly blond hair ahead. *Ah, yes. Him.*

He was talking to Slade and those guys. He said something that made them laugh. They were easier to see for a moment—those guys are usually so stuck about with hang-ups it's quite painful to look at them. But when the veils of fear and bad home life and wanting-a-red-car clustered back around them, Keenoy Ribson was still clear and unobscured. My eyes searched around him automatically, wondering where he hid all his stuff—some people can do that—searching and searching and finding nothing. Nothing at all. It was kind of stunning, like a fine day after a long rainy spell. I watched him closely—his relaxed walk, his personal version of the school uniform, the beaten-up school bag with his old school's crest on it, with the motto KNOW THYSELF—and I waited for interference, but he stayed as crisp and clean-edged as a photograph.

Several times that day I saw him, always with totally different groups of people. He didn't seem to care who he was seen with, Slade's roughnecks or Mandy's knitting circle or that nerd Purtwee. He always looked perfectly comfortable; the group was always cheerful and busy with conversation.

"Did you see that new guy?" I heard Josh Bateman

say. "What a suck—see him talking to Bannister? Getting in with the school captain . . . ?"

But at lunchtime there they were, Keenoy and Josh and all the soccer-heads together, out on the oval, kicking a ball around.

Nobody had a problem with him, unless you call the girls' instant wild crushes a problem. "*Such* a babe," Blossom O'Malley said to me—I happened to be standing near her when Keenoy walked past.

"You think?" I said.

"What, are you crazy?" She goggled at me.

"You think he's good-looking?"

She gazed after him. "Well, it's not so much the looks, though they're *okay*. It's more, he's so *happy*."

I liked Blossom for a second, then, with that note of longing in her voice. Just for that brief time, she had dignity, before all her usual cutesy, kittenish attachments bobbed in around her again.

| | | |

My work makes it hard for me to like people. They seem so despicable sometimes, going around inside out, all their weaknesses showing in their walk, in their clothes, in their I'm-in-control-of-it-all faces, let alone the visible holes in them, the baggage-people they drag around with them. Mum says these things are only obvious to me, though. I must remember, not everyone can see what's so shatteringly clear to me. I envy other people that, and I despise them. I can't see how they can live, so cluttered up with other people's lives and influences; I'd hate to live in someone else's shadow. Worse, I'd hate to go around with my insides all blurted out like that, moaning my wants to the whole world, mourning what I'd lost.

| | | |

Keenoy Ribson *went on* being happy. (I should've realised then, at least.) He didn't take on any of *our* hang-ups, didn't join any of the cliques. He seemed to enjoy himself, to enjoy being at *this* school, with *us*. He volunteered for the daggy old musical; he played sports—not well, but with lots of energy; he worked hard enough but didn't do brilliantly. And he talked. He greeted everyone, he chatted, he joked, he had deep-and-meaningfuls when deep-and-meaningfuls were required. He was always in there with people, close up, interacting.

I kept waiting for some insufficiency, some little longing, to show itself near him, but it never did. I'd have to talk to him, maybe, get to know him better, or just get him away from the crowd and see him against a plain background, before I'd know for sure.

I did follow him home one day—well, not all the way home. Somehow I lost him near the freeway overpass, just got distracted for the second it took him to disappear up some lane or into some house.

I didn't try again. I wasn't exactly in a hurry to be disappointed. (Funny how, through the whole thing, I always expected disappointment, even though I went after hope. "Went after"—hmph. I sat like a lump, doing nothing, letting hope grow all by itself, like ivy, latching onto me with its millions of little suckers.)

| | | |

"How does it come to you, the Knowledge?" one of my clients once asked me, a client who'd pulled a whole bunch of mooing, chattering gurus into the parlour with her, all their tethers snarled together.

It always annoys me, that soft, awed tone of voice. I sighed. "It's very simple. You know how some people have been hurt so badly that they shuffle when they walk, or they hunch over and hug the inside edge of the pavement? You know how angry people wear this angry face around all the time, with the pulled-down mouth and the eyes kind of flashing to warn you?"

"Yes, you're right!" She sounded surprised, as if this was new to her. "It's as if their experiences are imprinted in their bodies somehow."

"Well, exactly. And all you have to do is look a little bit closer, and all the details of that imprint will show you the shape of the thing that's giving them pain, or anger, or sadness. Usually it's another person, but it can be some *thing* they want badly, like a big house or a pile of gold— that can push you out of shape, too."

But I'd lost her—she'd gone all reverent again. She wanted me to be another guru, the guru of gurus, to give her the final answer that would pull all the others together into one simple rule for living. "It's a wonderful gift." She thought she was agreeing, but she was actually preventing herself from seeing. People do this *all the time*.

No, it's not a gift. Anyone can do it—but nobody does. Nobody bothers to read, from the way a person's spine bends or the way their voice turns all feathery when they're stressed, the shape of the *other* person who stands behind, or over, or inside, or squashed underneath the client. *Absent ones*, Mum calls them, but in fact they're very present. They've carved themselves into each client—sometimes gently and in a good way, sometimes with a single thump or shout spoiling a life, cramping every movement from that moment on. Just open your eyes and you'll see them.

| | | |

It was a Wednesday evening, getting into autumn. I was pushing Dad home from the park. Everything looked coldly blue, except for the golden interior of Bar Piccolo, like a little lantern between the closed minimart and the vacant shop that had once been the Bibliophile bookshop. Kids from school sat laughing around a table in there, among them Keenoy Ribson.

I guess I kind of loomed up to the window out of the dark, and Dad's wheelchair's a bit of an eye-catcher, and . . . anyway, Keenoy looked up, and lifted a hand as if we were old friends.

I put a smile on my face that died as soon as I was past the window. Then I heard footsteps, and there was Keenoy beside me. "Tess! I need a word with you."

"Oh?" I tried to casually hide the wheelchair behind me.

"Sorry. You in a hurry?" He indicated Dad with his eyes.

"Not really. Um, this is my dad."

"Hallo, Mr. Maxwell."

Dad's head wandered around to look at him.

"He's had a stroke," I said. "He can't speak." *In fact, he isn't really here at all. Please act as if he isn't here.*

"Ah." Keenoy nodded to him anyway. "I was just going to ask you, Tess. We're short one Beggar Maid in the musical. D'you think you could fill in the gap?"

Surprise made me laugh. "Hey, I'm not really performing material."

"All you have to do is sit in a bunch of Maids and sing a chorus, sway a bit. Nothing too hard."

"Sounds very *not* me."

He made a pleading face that I had to laugh at. "Come to rehearsal tomorrow," he begged. "Take a look."

"Okay, I'll take a look."

"Good *on* you!"

"I'm not promising anything."

"Look, you don't have to." He backed towards the café. "See you then."

He was gone. And I walked home smiling. Idiot.

| | | | |

I've made them sound really powerful, those "absent" ones. But in the end it's the clients who decide how helped, how timid, how lost they'll be. That's why I was so sour on making this thing of mine into a business. Before Dad died—sorry, had his stroke—I never would have dreamed of doing it. All I was doing, I felt, was taking money for telling people what they'd already spent *years* telling themselves—that Grandma was the only one who ever properly loved them, that she must be watching them from above, continuing to wish them well. Or that their dead child still lived *somewhere*—which it did, inside them—beaming innocence out into the world.

You want certain voices to speak to you—lovingly or bullyingly or whatever. You want it so badly that you throw them out from yourself, and when I hear them and repeat back to you what they say, it seems like proof. You forget it's your own ventriloquism, your own loss, your own hankering written into the space around you for just about anyone to read. I feel like a thief, charging you my fee, but if you need to hear, but won't listen for yourself, and if we need the money so badly, I'll do it. I won't like doing it, but I'll do it.

| | | |

I went home smiling and told myself not to get silly. I should have been tired, but I wasn't. Mum had lit a fire in the parlour fireplace, and I sat there with her for a while. In the firelight Dad looked like somebody's dreamy old grandpa, mesmerised by the flames, and Mum and I had a sleepy, bitsy conversation. I almost told her about the musical, but then I thought, *No, she'd be too delighted. She'd pin more on it than I want pinned . . . for now.* Instead, I let myself feel the occasional roll of excitement inside me, let Keenoy's face rise in my memory and shine across to me some of its happy light and warmth.

I went to the rehearsal next day. I volunteered straight up, and got parked among the Beggar Maids.

"Oh hi, Tess," said Zenardia. "I didn't know you were musical."

"Oh, I'm not. I'm only doing this as a favour to Keenoy." It was the first and last time I ever said his name, and it made a funny feeling in my mouth, a kind of embarrassing tang, as if I'd used a special, intimate name I had for him, loosed it in public.

But then the rehearsal started. It probably seems like nothing to a normal person, but I enjoyed myself. It was a silly, romantic story, interrupted by the soppiest songs, but I got caught up in it anyway. Everyone else was taking it so seriously! When Lexie Nelson, the main girl, was singing her duet with Keenoy, they were both so *excellent*, even standing there in their school uniforms, that I saw Lexie clearly for the first time. Her mother climbed down off her back and her pushy brothers faded away to nothing, and for several minutes she didn't care that Nick Stefanopoulos didn't love her the way she loved him. I sat there with all the other Maids—who'd stopped chatting to listen, just as impressed as I was—and I let myself think, *Maybe life could be like this.*

| | | |

Right back when I first discovered that other people didn't see what I saw, all I wanted to do was get out, climb down from this kind of princess's tower my knowledge puts me in, mingle, be with other people, act like them— unaware, laughing at my own mistakes. I can see that people's ignorance is blissful—I'd like to turn around and say to some clients, *Hey look, you'd be happier not knowing, Really, don't make me tell you.*

Because knowing is hard. For my clients, knowing just their own stuff is hard to cope with; for me, knowing everyone's . . . Well, I used *not* to cope; a school assembly used to make me pass out. Nowadays I can block out quite a bit of the noise and bother around people, but it still takes some strength to deal with, say, a half-full train carriage, where there's room for each person's burdens and yearnings to swell out and speak up and compete for attention. Whenever a new passenger climbs in, everyone's yearnings check out the new ones and then go back to their own blabbing and yowling. It gets exhausting. I only really have any peace when I'm on my own, shut away from everyone. The rest is . . . well, it'll always be hard work, won't it. I just have to face that.

| | | |

After the rehearsal, Keenoy walked me home. He was exactly the right height, just a bit taller than me. It makes me miserable now to think how perfect he was.

I told him everything. Well, he'd seen Dad, so he knew about all that, and he wanted to know more, and he asked about the stroke, and listened, and was sympathetic but not ghoulish about it. "That's hard on you and your mum." His tone of voice, of course, was righter than most people's, with no awkwardness in it. *He must have some kind of similar experience behind him*, I thought, *but where? If it hasn't left a mark on him, what's he done to get over it? What power does he have? What makes him so strong?*

I looked up at him occasionally as we walked and talked. His skin was totally spot-free, unmarked by freckles or acne or any other kind of imperfection. Blossom was right; it was a happy face. Happiness was built into it, the mouth always ready to smile if not actually smiling, the eyes kind of smallish but active, taking in everything and having a quick thought to match each taken-in thing. I liked him. For the first time in my life I could see how it was possible to like a boy, even for someone like me.

I didn't feel awkward at all, saying, "Would you like a hot drink or something?" when we reached my gate.

"Sure," he said.

I held open the gate after me. "Where do you live, anyway?"

"Just a little way along from here, really. Over Oaky Park way."

"Really? Why don't you go to Oaky Park High, then, instead of trawling all the way across here?"

"Oh, well, you know . . ."

I opened the door. Something went *crash!* in the kitchen. "So *clumsy!*" came Mum's voice, her really-upset voice. "You've turned into a baby—no, *worse* than a baby! You'll *never* grow up! You'll never be more than this clumsy wreck—"

I froze on the doorstep. Another crash. Sobbing.

Keenoy took my shoulders, moved me to one side and went in towards the kitchen. I started after him; I didn't want him to see, didn't want Mum to know he'd heard her losing it.

Dad was there, with food spilled down his shirtfront. Mum was down next to him, trying to scoop the mush on the floor back up into the bowl with a shaking spoon. She looked up and saw Keenoy—and recognised him. (Well, she would, wouldn't she?)

"I just wanted him to try," she said desperately. "Maybe he *could* feed himself! Maybe something's knitted back together in his head by now. Maybe he's healing in there and none of us can see it yet!" She said it all in a garbled, tear-hiccupped rush, while Keenoy took the bowl and spoon from her, put them in the sink, then turned back to put his arms around her—whoa! She was sobbing against him; she looked very small wrapped up in there, and he felt suddenly very big in the room. It seemed a big thing for a person to do, to comfort someone just because she needed it.

I stood by the door feeling sick. If it had been me, I would have concentrated on the mess: wiped up the mush, told Mum to sit down, made her a cup of tea, cleaned up Dad's shirt, moved around and around her and not touched her once, biting back my irritation. "I could have *told* you Dad would drop it! Don't you listen when I tell you? *He's not there!*" I never would have hugged her. I would have been too angry.

I went away, full of shame. I put my bag in my room, went into the parlour. Twenty minutes and my first client would be here. I'd have to calm down by then.

After a little while Keenoy Ribson came in. He stood in the doorway with a mug of hot chocolate in each hand, smiling.

"She okay?" I said gracelessly.

"She's fine. A 'momentary lapse,' she said. We all have 'em." He handed me a drink and sat down in the client chair.

"She'll never stop missing him. It's almost all she ever does."

"But not you?"

I tried to take a sip of my drink, but it gave my lip a warning scald. I blew on it instead. "Sure, I miss my dad. But that out there in the wheelchair, that's not him, and it never will be him. There's too much damage. I'm not going to fool myself."

"No, you're too clear-eyed for that." There was no sarcasm in his voice. He looked so singular and baggage-free in that chair, the chair I usually saw through such a fog of ghosts and inhibitions. For once, someone was looking at me to give me something, not to suck a reading out of me, not to be saved. He was looking, he was caring, he was interested. Nobody looks at me like that—and I'm not talking about romance here; this is so much more important than romance. *I'm so lonely in my life!* I remember thinking. *I've got no one!* What a sad novelty it was to confide in someone, to tell about just me. Usually people's sympathy locks straight onto Mum, and we all help and console her; I'm so competent and practical, it must seem like I don't need consoling.

"I've been meaning to ask you," I said—and it was a wonderful feeling, to be able to say anything I liked and know I wouldn't be laughed at, or revered—"Have you got a talent like mine?"

"Which talent's that? Like, of all your talents?" He raised his mug to me and took a sip. "I mean, I can sing, you heard me—"

"The talent of seeing . . . extra things about people."

"Extra things? What, like their potential as Beggar Maids?"

"Like their hang-ups."

"Their hang-ups?" And then he drank down his hot chocolate. In two gulps—I heard them both. He put the mug on the table next to the tissue box. His smile was a little strange, a little fixed.

"It's almost a psychic thing," I said, frowning from the empty mug to him. And despite that look in his eyes, which said clearly, *Don't go down this road,* I told him all about it, about my work, the things I see, and how he didn't fit into the system. Boy, did I blather on. "You don't even seem to have any parental pressure, which is crazy for a sixteen- or seventeen-year-old. Every other boy I know carries his father around on his back like a sack of cement—sometimes his mum's there, too, trying to heave off a bit of the dad's weight, trying to make life a bit easier. You don't seem to have anyone. Nothing gets to you; nothing pushes you out of your own shape. I don't see how that's possible. Are you some kind of strange non-grieving orphan? Have you got some kind of religious belief that clears all your gremlins away?" Blah, blah, blah.

When I finally shut up, he laughed gently. "You don't want to know, Tess."

"But I do! I'm *busting* to know! Because whatever you've got, I want it, too!" And I blah-ed on about that, too—clarity and self-assurance and kindness and—

He was still laughing. He was at his best-looking, laughing—maybe he was hoping that'd distract me.

But it didn't, and he laughed on, too long, too watchfully.

And then he slipped. His gaze flicked to the floor just for a second, and when he looked back to me his laughter had definitely turned nervous.

I looked down. I was trying to hide it from myself and see it at the same time, so the tether was very fine, disguising itself by following the pattern in the Turkish rug. But I knew that pattern; I could see where the line had to cross from one motif to another, wriggling through the pile like a snake through stubble. A thread of darkness ran from one side of the rug to the other, joining Keenoy's foot to mine.

"You idiot," I heard myself say.

Keenoy's smile was feebly apologetic now. His eyes wobbled, and then began to widen down his collapsing face, dragging the smile down with them.

"I *thought* you were too good to be true," I said, trying to save face.

Keenoy's head was a melted heap on his chest. His torso deflated with a wet *pop!*, his arms shrinking into his shoulders.

"You twit." I hit my head with my fist, over and over. "You sappy, cloth-brained, *stupid*—"

He was shrivelled to a tiny black blob on the end of the line, whipping back across the rug into the toe of my shoe. I hadn't noticed him leave, but now I felt him come back into me, like water-balloons bursting in my chest and throat. Then I was brim-full of my own self again, unhappy but unstretched, not yearning, not fooling myself.

I sat there for a bit, recovering. I could hear Mum humming along to the radio in the kitchen. Keenoy's empty mug sent up a last lazy curl of steam. I felt like a complete fool. But at least it was over now; I didn't have to wonder any more.

And then the front gate clicked open, letting my first client in. Taking a deep breath, I got up and went to the door.

| | | |

MIDSUMMER

ISSION

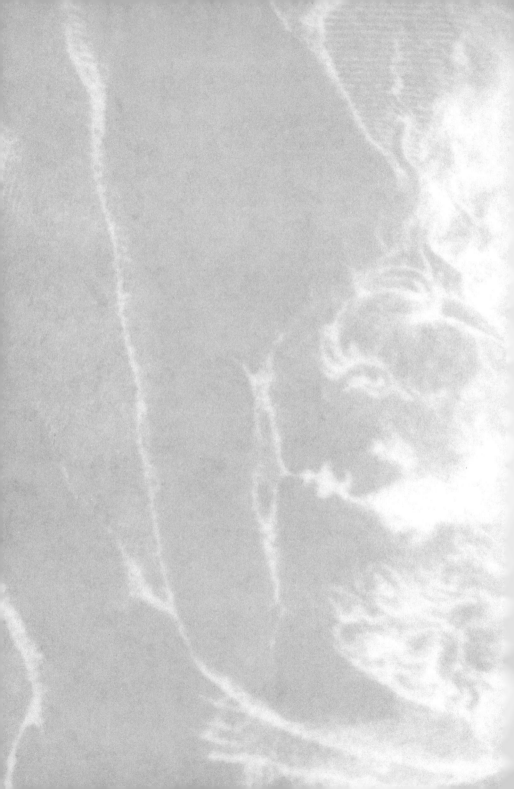

It was one o'clock in the morning. Streetlight gleamed into the empty classroom through venetian blinds. Above one of the desks, a pinpoint of elf-light was poised. It brightened, thrumming softly, and four tiny figures tumbled forth onto the desktop. The thrumming stopped, and the light winked out.

| | | |

"Gods dammit," said Hat. "Where in the flying fuck have they popped us?"

Snap whapped him with her cap. It had a hard-bell on it, and must have hurt. Hat pretended it didn't.

"In a Designated Place," said Motto, keeping himself po faced.

"Well, it's hot as hell. Slick as buggery, too—how's a snag supposed to get a purchase on this?" Hat stamped.

He was right, the ground was very hard and slippery. But I was heartened; I've heard of missionaries being popped through into water, into ovens, into unbounded snow.

"It has a pattern like our timber," said Snap, her bum in the air as she examined the ground. "Only *huge.*"

"Plateaus of polished jove-timber all around," I stated.

Hat snarled. "Oh, don't *suck*, Trinket."

I was stung, but I tried not to show it. "We'll all have to report when we get back, Hat."

"Report my hairy arse."

Motto turned away with beautifully practised Neutrality. Lovely to see. If only we could all do that.

"Airy plateaus," I continued, beginning to feel Virtuous, "ranked in rows as far as the eye can see. Cornered four-wise, many of them—"

"Oh, let's get *moving*, fuck it!"

"And where do you suggest?" snapped Snap.

I jumped in before Hat could answer. "The High Ones said it would be close. We should each go to one of the four edges of this plateau and assess the terrain below."

"Very good thinking, Trinket. Very ordered," said Motto.

Hat's grumbling and the tinkling of our cap-bells dispersed across the bare, smooth landscape. At the edge I lay down and looked over. The plateau stood on poles that went down and down to a dark, blank plain.

"Here!" cried Motto. "I believe I have it!"

We tapped across the timber to him, Snap doing little skids and whoops. "Careful," I said. "You'll go over." She stuck her tongue out at me.

We lay down either side of Motto. A blob of crumpled white paper lay on the plain below.

"Yep," said Snap. "Looks like a Map to me."

"Do you think?" said Motto enchantedly.

"Indeed, indeed," I said. I flung myself over the edge and unsnicked my thing-dang. The cord whipped up; the dang opened and began its slow whirl. I heard three snicks above me as the others followed.

Motto landed proudly right on the Map, and kept balance though the balled paper wobbled. His dang fed neatly down into his belt. "Give us your Hands here, Trinket," he said, beginning to crackle open the Map. "Ooh, I do have an excellent feeling about this!"

"'Tis very tightly crushed," I grunted, hauling on a wedge of it.

"'Tis very secret," he panted, "very *important*."

"You truly think?"

"Oh, yes. Here, look—there is Script on it! Keep opening. We must get it out flat. We are so lucky, to have no wind."

"Yes, indeed!" We had all heard those stories, of mission-maps snatched away into blowing snow, or caught in fire-draught—or worse, fires, and consumed.

"We will need light, however," said Motto. "Snap? Where is Hat? We must make light."

Snap started, and peered through the dimness. "Hat? Come and do your duty!"

"Hush," I said. "There may be Rats."

Hat's voice came faintly. "I'm busy. Busy dying of hunger, I am." He was just visible, ambling towards us, his feet catching in the ground's whiskery weave.

"He's stalling," I said. "Tsk, tsk."

Snap snarled. "The snot-head. I'll jump him."

"Is that Procedure?" I warned.

"Bugger that. You heard Motto—we need light."

She ran off. I saw her knock Hat down and quickly do the deed on him. I clicked my tongue some more and shook my head.

She came back groaning flamboyantly.

"Sshh! Remember! *Rats!*" I hissed.

"Trinket, go and shit in your cap, would you? Can you *smell* any Rat?" She sat down and held her belly. "Aah. Hooh. Haa."

Hat came up scowling, clipping the belt of his green-pants. "Bugger you blind, you minx. Did you see what she did?"

"Ha!" said Snap. "Milking you for light's what I'm here for, Hat. And you're here to be milked." She opened her shirt to make way for her swelling belly.

"You're just a hot-pot, that's your trouble," said Hat.

Motto and I had the Map undone. It was finely striped, proper Script-paper, with a single line of Script across the middle. "Look at this rough edge," I said. "Maybe it is torn from a larger map?"

"But the Script is all constrained to the middle," said Motto. "So I do not think we are missing any. This is excellent. How goes it, Snap?"

"Hoo. Hoo. Hoo—Very well—hoo—"

"Can we eat, while we wait?" said Hat.

"Not and keep to Procedure," said Motto.

"Fuck Procedure's eyes. I need food. Popping takes it out of a person."

"Nevertheless." Motto was crawling all over the Map, and rolling to flatten it.

Snap's whole front glowed yellow. "Here we go. Here we go—" A dot of bright light appeared on her belly, and opened out round and wide. "Ah!" She forced out the light-globule. Her belly snapped closed and she panted, her eyes shining. "It's a beauty."

"Over here," said Motto. The light flew gently to him, and he whistled. "*Very* clear Script, Trinket. No erasures or obliterations."

"Can you get a general sense of it?" I said.

"Passion. Care. Those are the immediate possibilities."

We stood around waiting. "So lucky, with this quietness," I murmured. Hat's stomach burtled, making the silence pointed. The light-globe backed and forthed over the crinkled Script-paper, stretching and shrinking shadows. The Script began to tangle and shine, to swell and show its Essence. It heaped up on the paper in tangling skeins of red and gold and purple light.

"Now *there's* a Passion for you," said Motto.

"Which one is it?" Even Hat was impressed.

Snap snorted. "I think it's fairly clearly Love, Hat."

"That's Love? Bugger it—I wanted something with *Mischief* in it."

"And what about these other pieces?" I asked Motto. Two groups of Script at either end of the Love-mound had formed flatter, duller mounds of interwoven shapes. "They look like High Ones' belt-buckles."

"Light-seed to a *Love*-mission!" moaned Hat. "How will I ever live it down?"

Motto cleared his throat. "Well, Trinket, those would have to be the names of the two parties. Pretty, don't you think?"

"Mm. What are they?"

He shielded his eyes against the Love's light. "This one is . . . Lee-sah. And over here . . . Naw-bair. With the positioning of them, the Love flows from Leesah to Nawbair. You can even see it." And indeed there did seem to be some light streaming from the Love-mound towards Nawbair's name-shape.

Motto walked around on the Map, eyeing the Script from all sides. He took off his cap and made scratch lines all over his scalp. The light-globe was beginning to fade now, but the Love's Essence and the two names beamed shifting colours up into our faces. The streaming was now quite clear, tatters of light blowing loose from the main mound and over the Nawbair name.

"I think what we have here," said Motto, "is a classic mission of Correcting an Imbalance—"

"Oh, spare us the goose-shite. What do we *do*?" said Hat.

Snap pushed him. "Let Motto *say*!"

Motto was looking miffed.

"So we must stop this streaming?" I asked.

He replaced his cap, flicked his ear-tips out from under it, and folded his arms. "On the contrary, I think we must Evoke some streaming from the other side also."

"Some Love must flow from Nawbair to Leesah, you mean?" said Snap.

"Precisely. So we must Influence Nawbair."

"And can you draw a bead on this jove?" said Hat, then moaned softly, "I'm so *hungry*."

"Oh, for gods' sake," said Snap, "can we give him some waypork? And I know that's not *Procedure*." She rolled her eyes at me.

"We cannot," I said. "Not if popping is required. Be quiet now while we establish it."

"You are such a bloody *suckhole*, Trinket!" said Hat.

"Shut up!" said Snap. "She's just doing her job."

Motto knelt beside Nawbair's name and described Signs with his hands. One day I might be able to do half as good work, but I would never have such fine hands for it. His were special and delicate; mine were just Hand hands, for blunt work.

He spread his bony fingers above the name, and his narrowed eyes went sightless. "He is not anywhere nearby. We will definitely have to pop."

"Fuck and *fuck* it again. How far?"

"Ooh! Quite far. He does not live here; this is some kind of daily prison we are in."

"A prison?" Snap looked around fearfully.

"Yes, but the prisoners may go to their homes to sleep and eat, also to change their clothing and to be with parents—although they do not enjoy that."

"It sounds as if you have a good fix on him, Motto," I said.

"Oh, yes. He is at home and sleeping now, very deeply. Now would be a good time to pop in."

"We will want to come back here afterwards?"

"Yes please, Trinket. Or to wherever this Map blows if a wind should spring up."

"I'll hold it down," said Hat. "Leave me and some pork and I'll keep it in place while you go and Influence."

"Oh, Hat, you know that's not how it's done," said Snap.

I got out my pot of sticky and put a glom on the Map to mark it. "Very well, then, let's go."

First I, then Snap, and finally Hat hooked ourselves backways to Motto.

"Have you drawn the bead, Motto?" I asked.

"I'm right on the jove and holding."

We closed our eyes and popped. This time there was less spangling and wooziness, but when we were spat out behind the jove's head we still had to fall apart and breathe a little.

"Whoo!" said Snap.

"This is softer." I poked at the pushy, pale ground. "Fabricked. This must be one of those 'pilloes.'"

"State the fucking obvious, why don't you?" Hat rolled onto all fours and retched.

I caught Snap's eye. "Just think, now, if we'd given him pork." She looked away queasily.

"We'll need another light," said Motto.

"*I* can see!" said Hat hurriedly, between groans. "I can see to put a snag up, easy!"

"Can we wait some?" said Snap.

"Speediness is next to goddishness," said Motto. I was getting a little tired of his Virtue. "How are you, Trinket?"

"Ready to do my duty." I jumped to attention.

"Go to it, then."

"Ah." I realised what I had said. "Well, get up, Hat."

"Unh?"

"We must do the deed, for light."

"But I can *see*!"

"Do it, Trinket," said Motto. "Let's not waste time."

"Under orders," I apologised as I booted Hat onto his back. I did the deed on him quite slowly, for a good long light in case anything should go wrong. He groaned and coughed underneath me all the while.

I walked away to bring forth the light-globule; I don't like to be watched for that sort of thing, especially by people in a hurry. When it came out, it was worth all the groaning and stretching, it was so big and intense. I had never seen a light so good, myself.

"Right. Snagging time. Go, Hat." Motto was a-sheen with energy.

"Yeah, yeah." Hat unlooped the snag and threw it up to the jove's ear; we all scrambled up the cord, the hair wiry and warm underfoot.

"In there?" I eyed the dark ear-hole with its fancy door.

"'Tis the best place for Influence," said Motto.

"We won't all fit in there."

"Only I will go. I will not need a Hand for this part of the mission."

We sat about in the hair-grass as he prepared. He took the starry cap with the silver bell from its satchel with a lovely Reverence, and when he put it on he looked properly High and wizardly. He took the Sphere from its velvet and gently polished it ready, then rewrapped it and tucked it back inside his shirt.

"Can we eat now?" said Hat.

Snap smacked him. "Watch and learn," she said.

"Aaarrgh. I'll eat *him* in a minute."

"Sshh!"

"Be utterly quiet now," said Motto, and lowered himself into the hole. I sat on a part of the rim that formed a natural, slightly bristly seat. The whole place had a curious earthen smell about it.

Motto gave a little squeak and his fingertips disappeared from the rim. What—the head was hollow? I scrambled forward. No, there he was, just down there. The stars and moons on his cap gleamed as the light-globe shifted around behind me. Motto did not look up he was already settling into his Mood.

He took out the Sphere, unwrapped it, held it on its cloth and began to chant. Oh, he was very good, swift but solemn, tossing off the crisp consonants and the reverberant vowels of mage-speak as if he had spoken them since birth.

The Sphere responded, appearing to explode slightly into a puff of Love-light in his hands, mauve and yellow with touches of red, snaking around on itself. He talked the Influence fuzzier at the edges, and larger. It swelled to encompass his own head, then filled the ear-hole to brimming with tangling brightness. Motto's chant came up through it without hesitation or strain. I sat back as the light began to swell out. I could not help smiling at Motto's sure touch—and on our first mission!—and at the beauty of this thing he was working.

"Aargh!" Hat said behind me. "How long's this going to *take?*"

There was no time to answer this rudeness, for a terrible convulsion shook the jove-head and tumbled me off the ear-door. I grabbed some hair to stop myself being flung farther.

"Fuck me dead and blind!" shouted Hat from somewhere on the far side of the ear.

The light-globe darted away. A vast jove-hand came at the ear, squashed the puff of Love there, fingered the hole with a concentrated roughness, and went away. Shreds of torn Passion floated off and faded on the darkness. I lay there clinging. "Motto. Motto!" He could not survive that, surely?

Then the whole world began to tumble. I was thrown off the head and rolled and rolled. Only quick action with my snag stopped me flying off the sleeping-plateau.

Nawbair's head had turned right over, and re-settled. I stood up aghast, my snag still in the ground-fabric in case of another convulsion.

I heard a frightened muttering in the folds to my right. "Dags and bleeding dildoes. Fuck the gods and their whims. Who gives a gobbet of goose-shite whether he Loves her back or not?"

"Snap is all right?" I called.

"Snap's gone I don't know where." Hat clambered into view. I straightened up and looked around—and saw nothing but the jove's giant face, with its whistling nose, rushing mouth and vast, lidded eyes.

"Did Motto happen to fly out?" said Hat.

"I didn't see him. I saw a finger mash him and then I was thrown off."

"Mash him?" Hat's ear-tips flattened to the side of his head. "You saw the mash?"

"No, only the finger. But he must be mash, it was so

ferocious. I hadn't thought a sleeping jove could do that."

"Nor I." Hat looked sick. "Oh, my. Have we lost him, then?"

"I think we must have."

"Aagh." He held his head; his cap-bell fell forward with a tinkle. "And all I could think of was my stomach! What kind of missionary am I?"

"I'd have thought Snap would crawl out from somewhere by now," I said.

Hat held his cheeks, staring at me. "Did she fall past you and off the pillo?"

"I didn't see her."

"She was still hanging on when I fell off—gods strike me!" He turned and gazed in horror at the jove's great head.

We crept towards it, clutching each other, skirting the breeze-ways. The light-globe came down and hovered nervously above us.

Then Hat gave a whimpering cry and flung himself on me. "Ah, Trinket! No, don't look! She is elf-mash! The god has her!"

"Hie. Hie. Calm down. Stop it, Hat. Hat!"

I managed to calm him to only loud weeping; then I pushed him aside and went forward. The light-globe was trembling by the jove's eyelid. From under the massive head, among the wiry eyelashes, a tiny hand projected.

Shakily I knelt. "It has not been much time, though," I muttered, and reached in and stroked the limp fingers. "And the ground is very soft. There may be a chance—" I reached for my sticky-pot. "Hat! I need you, and quickly!"

He came up sniffling. "How?"

"You must pull her out, when I lift the head."

"Lift it? You can do that, with sticky?"

"Of course." I had never lifted anything this big, but my hands were scooping out sticky as if they knew it would work. And what else could I do? I was no kind of mage.

I knew not to sticky the eyelid; that would only lift the lid. But that was about all I knew. I used up all the sticky I had, glomming it thickly along the cheek and brow bones—and wished I had just a little bit more, to be sure.

"All right? You are ready, Hat? Get in close and be holding the hand. You will only have a tiny moment."

He nodded, swollen-eyed, and crouched in among the eyelash wires.

I took and released a preparatory breath. Then I said a quick, clear prayer of Concentration, bowed, and waited for the sticky to blow.

Thump. Thick, grey smoke shot away from the giant face. The head didn't move much, but it *did* move. Then I breathed in some choking sticky-smoke, and had to stagger clear. Sickly, coughing, I watched the light-globe dancing, unable to light much in the smoke.

Finally Hat came, dragging Snap's body, coughing into his sleeve. He got her into clear air, and we threw ourselves on our knees beside her. I slapped her cheeks, shook the point of her chin. "Snap! Are you there?"

"Arruggff," she said finally, and her eyes fluttered open.

"Oh, Snap!" wept Hat, tearing off his cap and flinging himself on her chest. "I thought you were mash! I thought we would never see you again!"

"Get off, you great lump," I said, pushing at him. "She may be broken!"

"I'm not," she said, blinking and vaguely patting Hat's black-straw hair. "But let me breathe."

"But I was so frightened! When that bastard jove lay on you, and your little hand was sticking out—oh, Snap! I'm so sorry!"

"Oh, for gods' sake, Hat!" I stood up and tried to kick him off, but he was built like a stove-tank and all I did was hurt my toes on his great bum.

Snap laughed weakly. "It's all right, Trinket."

"It is *not*. We are right by a jove's face, and must get out of here, must get home and report our mission's failure."

There was sudden silence. "I don't care about the mission," Hat said softly into Snap's face, her hand clutched to his chest. "As long as you are still with us."

"But Motto?" Snap said to me dazedly.

I shook my head.

She pulled her hand free of Hat's and sat up. "Oh. Oh. This is serious."

"Let her up, Hat. We must pop back."

Right then a great Magic began to buzz the air all around. Hat screamed and hauled Snap up and away, and I ran after them. We snagged ourselves behind a pillo-hillock.

"Are the High Ones intervening?" said Snap.

"No, it's coming from the jove," said Hat.

Was it? I moved my head around, listening. "I think you're right," I said in astonishment. "It must be Motto."

"Motto?" said Hat. They stared at me. "Didn't you say he was mashed?"

"Motto could do that?" shouted Snap above the increasing noise.

The jove-head began to shimmer, then to crawl all

over with light, tiny patterns at first, like dust motes swimming, then growing until the head was like a squirming ball of elvers, blood-red and bruise-purple, shooting flashes of gold. The air thrummed and zithered.

"What's he *doing*?" Snap screamed in my ear. "Isn't that Love-light?"

I nodded, unable to tear my eyes away from Motto's creation.

"But what will that do to the jove?"

It woke the jove up.

Nawbair's eyes opened, beaming gold from the light-mess that was his face. He looked straight at us, and even though he did not see us, I was glad I had no waypork in my stomach, for it would have ended up in my green-pants then and there. The whole pillo quaked and we were flung about like lace bobbins on the ends of our snag-strings.

And Nawbair got up. The white-hot Sphere of Influence fell out of his ear, followed by Motto. The air of the giant's rising sucked them sideways off the pillo. Motto bounced, twice, on the sleeping-plateau. Nawbair stood and took his swirling head away, well away, and sat down at a distant table, and set a jove-light burning there.

Snap unsnagged herself and ran. Hat and I went after her. Motto was scrambling after the bouncing Sphere, trying to catch it in its velvet and avoid the small fires it was starting all along the ground.

"Motto!" I cried, stamping on one of them. "Dazzling work—most impressive!"

"It was only to save my skin." Finally he trapped the Sphere with the velvet. He sat wrapping and rewrapping it, quenching its heat. "I will be in serious trouble for that."

"How so?" Snap jumped spread-legged, squashing two sparks out under separate shoon.

"I have not Redressed a Balance." He looked up at us and shrugged. "I have created a worse *Im*balance. I have committed an Interference."

"Can nothing be done?" I said. "Can we not pop over to Leesah's place and balance her Passion with his?"

Motto shook his head vehemently. "We must touch nothing. Procedure says. We must go home and report, and let higher ones than us determine whether anything can be done."

"Thank gods," said Hat, rolling on the last spot fire. "Let's go."

Motto caught and quenched my light-globe in the Sphere's velvet. In the distance, Nawbair's teeming head was bent over some work on the table.

We hooked ourselves together and popped—and landed in a blaze of Love-light, with the ground crackling under us.

"Fuck me *over*!"

"It's the Map!" I cried. "I stickied it for our return, remember?"

We all tried to roll different ways; Hat prevailed in the end.

"Jove take me, look at that!" said Snap.

The mound of Love was enormous. It was still streaming towards Nawbair's name, but I could only see that if I put up my hand to block out the white flare of Passion howling the other way.

"Don't unhook!" I said. "We will all pop straight on."

"No." Motto unhooked himself. "I must bring this."

"But we must bring nothing!" I cried. "We were expressly told—"

"We must show the High Ones what we have done." And he stamped through the Love-mound, making a crease in the Map. Little squirts of Love-light came out as he folded the paper flat.

"It's a monster you've made," said Snap in fearful wonder.

"You don't need to tell me," gloomed Motto. He backed up to us with the bulky Map in his arms, and we helped hook him in.

"One last pop, Hat, and then you can eat," I said.

"Urgh," he said. "Don't talk about it."

We closed our eyes and popped.

| | | |

It was almost dawn. Norbert Pendle, a thick wad of love letter tucked into his shirt, crouched in the shrubbery in front of Lisa Tully's house. Which window was hers? He thought he'd go mad, not knowing. When he did find out, he'd climb up to it every night. He'd leave gifts on the sill—roses, letters, beautiful feathers; he'd save up his pocket money and buy her a ring. Or he'd *climb in!*, and just sit by her bed and watch her sleeping, watch her beautiful sleeping face.

He laughed aloud. Beautiful? Until that dream last night, he hadn't noticed her beauty, hadn't ever cast her a second look. He hated his own stupidity; he growled and scratched savagely at the rash on his cheekbone as if to punish himself. But now he knew: Lisa Tully was beautiful, outside and in—strangely graceful, she was, deceptively quiet, quite inappropriately modest. The eczema blooming on the insides of her elbows showed there was passion trapped inside her, a high intelligence bursting to free itself. He, Norbert Pendle, would be the one to release it. He knew this more clearly than he'd ever known anything.

Yesterday's heat and pollution still lay across the suburbs, a blanket that couldn't be kicked off. A milkfloat turned into Lisa's street and laboured up the hill, its load giving off a chilled, glassy rattle. Two bushes away, a bird protested weakly against the coming of day. Norbert noticed nothing; he hugged his knees in a fever of Love, shivering and burning with it. He had never been so happy.

| | | |

WELCOME
BLUE

This guy Quaid, he seems okay. He hasn't belted me yet, or done anything creepy. Last night he just said, "Early start tomorrow," and this morning, "Up you get, Eleanor." Which was good—it's best when they've got something for you to do besides sit around wishing you weren't here. That's why kids like me go off the rails—from boredom more than anything else.

The sky's getting light now, but down here it's still dark. Skinny gum trees rush out of the dark and then slide off sideways out of the Four-By utility's headlights.

Then there's a gate across the road. "Get that, would you?" Quaid says. I figure out the door-catch and hop out, nervous. I don't know why—like, this's such a big test? It means unlooping some chain and walking the gate wide open. It means waiting while he drives through, with the cold chewing on my face. It means walking the gate closed and re-hooking the chain. There, that wasn't too much of a stretch, was it?

Nothing's said when I hop back in the cab. No "positive reinforcement," no little silver bows. This isn't a silver-bow-type guy. I don't know what kind of guy he is, besides old.

We bowl along. At least the road's straighter now and I can stop having to hold down Mrs. Quaid's big, eggy breakfast. But it's weird to be up so early. I didn't sleep all that well—never do, first night somewhere new. Especially somewhere so neat, in a room on my own, a room full of girl things left over from their daughter—who's got daughters herself now, and sons, two of each, Mrs. Quaid told me. Not that I asked. I never ask. If they don't ask about me, I don't ask about them—that's my policy.

We come around a bend and the big main street of town is all lit up. There's a banner hanging slack under every street lamp: WELCOME! WELCOME! on both sides of the road. I turn around to look out the back at their other sides—and they say WELCOME! WELCOME! too, left and right, all the way back down the street.

"Huh! Nice of everybody," I joke. "The big welcome."

Quaid doesn't say anything—he's gunning it, squinting out past the lights.

We fly past the Town Hall. Boy, is it tizzed up. WELCOME! it shouts, to no one. The pillars out front are all wound around with flowers; there are streamers and balloons and fancy painted wooden borders dressing up the windows. "Who's coming, the Queen?"

Quaid says nothing.

Then I notice a lot of the houses are decorated, too. Some people have gone the whole hog and streamered up their front fences and verandas and that; others have just got a thing like a pale Christmas wreath on the gate or the front door. It's hard to get a proper look at one as we whizz by, but they seem to be made of paper flowers, with a white ribbon across the middle, with gold writing on it.

We go on out of town. Everything's dark and normal for a while, just those white posts with the little reflectors flicking by, white to the left, red to the right. Then we pass a turn-off with a sign, SHOWGROUND, and I can see the showground off to the right, because the whole thing's brighter than daylight from these humungous blazing floodlights.

"What's going on there?" The place is crawling. The car park's full and a nearby field is stuffed with cars, too. There are tents. There are a couple of grandstands full of people, and down on the empty oval people are crowding, too, hundreds of them. "What is it, a circus?"

Quaid snorts. "Could say that." He's not even looking.

"Funny time to hold it," I say suspiciously. "Before sunrise?" He doesn't move or answer.

Well, great. I'm probably missing the only interesting thing to happen around here this decade. That'd be right.

I start to be able to see things out the window: bitten-down fields, sheep that look like rocks, rocks that look like sheep, a pale little skinny lamb every now and again. *Cold-looking dams, their banks worn bare by sheep hooves, sad-looking trees hanging over them, dark houses with empty carports beside. This's so *not* my kind of place. I don't know how to start *thinking* about how to act here.

Quaid slows, and turns off the road. A gate. We sit there a moment before I realise I'm supposed to open it.

It's still cold. In a clump of trees some birds are making quiet squarkling noises.

I hop back into the Four-By and we jounce across an empty field—another gate. Just past it there's a metal shed with a wide veranda along the back, and behind the shed is Quaid's crop.

"Oh," I say as he gets out of the cab. "These were all through the town."

"No, they weren't." He slams the door.

I get out and go around the cab. "Yeah, they were—on everyone's doors, didn't you see?"

"Not these ones."

I follow him to the shed. "No, not *these* ones. This kind of flower, is what I meant."

He rolls up the shed door. Inside there's a stack of boxes, long, flat, and narrow. Beside them, brown packets—Quaid rips open the top one, pulls out a piece of purple tissue paper and lays it in a box. "Come and I'll show you the drill." On the way out he takes down one of a few big hook-ended knives by the door. He puts the box down by the front row of crop, which is lit up by the Four-By's lights.

"You want about this much stem," he says. "Take orf about five at a time—'bout that thick, you want the blooms. Knife *away* from you, every time, see? Then, into the box—gently. Then another five—pack the flowers the other end . . . and that's your box full. See them trolleys? You fill 'em up with the empty boxes, all open, all lined, and pull 'em along the rows with you."

It isn't hard, just boring. The flowers look nice, though they don't have a smell. Probably just as well, 'cause there's a heck of a lot of them; it might be a bit much on a full stomach. But it doesn't hurt, and I don't stuff up, and Old Man Quaid leaves me alone, which is more than I can say for some bosses I've had. He comes by and checks a few boxes, and goes off again without swearing at me. He's not one of those men who has to show he's the boss all the time. He works unbelievably fast; I get faster than I was at the start, but nowhere near as fast as him. He doesn't seem to be hurrying, but the rows empty behind him, the boxes stack up.

As it gets lighter, some traffic comes by. There's an old bus, crammed with people singing. A pale-purple flag flies out behind it, and mauve and white streamers are trailing out the windows. When the passengers see us they start whooping and calling out. Hands stick out the windows and wave. Quaid eases his back and watches them go by, but he doesn't wave back, or smile, or anything. So neither do I.

On we work. It's so quiet. I can hear Quaid breathing half a field away; I can hear his knife slicing, *shlook*!, through the stalks, as if he was right next to me.

Then a ute comes by, a Four-By like Quaid's only

newer, freshly resprayed. Resprayed pale purple, with groovy white transfers skedaddling up the side of the cab. It slows down. The white-shirted driver hooks his arm out the window and grins.

"Hey, Quaid! Wanna lift inna town?"

I look down the row. Quaid's working away as if he didn't hear a word.

"Who's 'is girlfriend?" says some idiot in the cab.

"Hey, Quaid! Who's ya girlfriend?" The driver looks me up and down. I glare back, in between cutting two fives of flowers.

There's a burst of laughter from the ute. "Well, you'll miss the biggest thing ever happened here, mate!" the man shouts to Quaid, and they drive off.

Almost straight away I hear another car in the distance. This one's long and low and black. It slows down as it goes past, then stops, and backs up. The back windows are dark so you can't see in.

"Oh, *far* out," I mutter. But this driver sits looking straight ahead. He wears a black hat with a shiny peak to it, like some sort of army officer, and black leather gloves.

"Girl? Excuse me, girl!"

A woman's getting out of the back. She's wearing a straight, elegant dress, knee-length, mauve, and strappy mauve high-heel sandals. She totters across the road and makes a girly little hop across the ditch.

"I was just wondering if I might have some of your flowers," she says. "Just what you have there would be marvellous."

She seems so sure of herself that I take a step towards her. Then I pause. "They're not mine," I say. "You'll have to ask the boss." Who's cutting and packing with his back to us.

"Oh, must I?" I stare back at her and her face turns cranky. "Go on, then—fetch him over."

Quaid seems to be stubbornly not turning round to see me as I step through the rows of chopped stems. "Um . . . Mr. Quaid?" I say when I think he must be able to hear me. He doesn't respond. Maybe he's a bit deaf, being so old?

I stand beside him feeling as if I'm talking to myself. "There's a lady there . . . wants to know if she can have a five of flowers . . ."

He shakes his head, just the tiniest shake.

"No?"

He goes on working. Six fives lie down in the boxes in the few seconds I wait.

I take a deep breath. "Okay." I turn and go back over the chopped rows.

"I'm sorry," I say to the mauve lady. "He says no."

"But you've got *millions* here! You can spare five! Just—those ones in your hand will be gorgeous. Just pass *them* over!"

"I have to do what he says. And he'll see. They're his flowers. I can't—"

"Oh, for goodness' sake—Mr. Quaid!" she cries, making me jump. "Could I have a word with you!"

Quaid turns as if he's only just realised she's there. He takes his time coming over—all of a sudden he's old-codgerish, pausing to hook out a weed and checking the ground in front of every footfall.

"Mrs. Allan," he says when he's still a fair way off.

"What a gorgeous crop you have this year!" She's pretty good with the smile; she looks really admiring.

"Oh, it'll pay for some bad years, I reckon." His voice sounds very soft and far away after hers.

"I was wondering if you could spare me just the tiniest bunch for today's celebrations—they're so suitable for a welcoming!"

Even from here, I can see that Quaid's eyes look like little steel buttons.

The silly cow gushes on, "*Exactly* the shade! And so fresh and lovely looking." Her voice shakes a little at the end.

Quaid lets the sound hang there for about a minute. "Well, I've heard Henny Barbier's grown quite a few for today's purposes. And they're not difficult to grow in a home garden. You should have your man Thrushton put in a few in a nice sunny place with a bit of rich soil, bit of compost . . ."

"Oh, but—well, I would have, but I was in Milan when it was time to be doing that sort of thing, you see."

"There is the telephone, Mrs. Allan, and the letter post, and these days—Mr. Allan's got a computer, hasn't he? I hear these computers can talk to each other, across the world."

"*Call* it an oversight," she begs, clutching the barbed wire. Ooh, her fingernails are frosted mauve, and lo-ong. Perfect. Her lips are mauve, her stockings, her eye frost! She's so *coated*, so finished off. She looks really *weird* standing next to the weathered fence post. "Just *three* little stalks, Mr. Quaid. Surely that won't impoverish you? Look, I can *pay* you! I'd be happy to pay you! How would that be?" She makes to dart back over the ditch.

Quaid's flat voice stops her. "And the minute you do that, I'll have a roadside stall on my hands, and this staff making change when she could be cutting."

Ooh. "This staff" means *me*. My chin goes up. *Yeah, so put that in your pipe, lady.*

"But I won't tell a *soul*, I *promise*—"

"It won't make a difference; they'll know these are Quaid's blooms. People've been passing 'em for weeks. Now you take yourself and your flash car orf from here. I never wanted any of these blooms down there at today's nonsense and I don't want it now."

Her face darkens so that her mauvish make-up sits on it like maybe a dust, or some kind of thin fur. She turns back and clutches the spiky top of the fence post. "It may be nonsense to *you*, Mr. Quaid, but it's other people's *beliefs*, their deepest, most heartfelt *beliefs*, that you're dismissing so lightly."

"Well, they're welcome to 'em, is all I can say, ma'am. Come on, Eleanor, let's get on with it."

"You're a very cold man, Mr. Quaid." She's going to *cry*! "When the gods come down to our little community today, I hope they spare you a glance, up here on your own, worshipping your money, withholding your welcome. I hope their hearts are bigger than yours!"

He's not even really looking at her. "You get as old as me, Mrs. Allan, you realise everyone's heart's pretty much the same size."

And he turns away and goes back down the field. I take a last glimpse of loony Mrs. Allan, her face red, her shoulders hunched, and I put my handful of flowers in their box. I'm glad I'm me and not the guy in her car; I'm glad I'm not *her* staff.

I cut and pack and trolley and stack boxes into cartons. The sun comes up over the hill; it brings the faint smell of sap out of the chopped stalks. The air's so fresh, the sun's so bright—there's a breeze, though, so I never get hot, even though my whole body is moving, bending, steering the trolley. It's okay, I realise. If I did this work all day every day, it might be okay for a while.

There's quite a lot of traffic at midmorning, car-loads and bus-loads heading into town. Some are all purple and white, others just ordinary. No one else stops and tries to buy flowers, although everyone seems to *look* very hard at them as they swish by.

Towards noon, this cool little red and white *aeroplane* comes and lands in the empty field next to the crop, and collects all the boxes of flowers we've picked. "Where's he taking them?" I ask Quaid, watching the plane soar away again.

"Airport in the city. Then Japan. Japan and California, mostly."

"Wow!" I look at the crop with new eyes. "I never thought these would be for . . . for Japanese and Californian people."

"Makes a difference, does it?" says Quaid mildly. "May as well have a break now, eh. Then we'll get back to it."

I follow him to the veranda. The field seems really quiet after the plane. There are bird calls and insect shrills, but there are no engines, no people, no music—only a thick, felty silence underneath all the little noises.

Quaid opens the esky. There's bread and cheese, some kind of salami, big green pickles. There's chilled fruit, and freezing-cold water to drink. I'm in heaven, sitting on an upturned milk crate eating that lunch, outside but in the shade, covered in cool sweat. I'll get tired of it one day, maybe, but right now it's all new and good.

"We haven't done much," I say. "Not when you look at how much there's left."

Quaid chews and swallows. "It's seventy rows we don't have to do again."

The breeze is in among the flowers; they sway and flow but never move on. The sunlight's so bright on them they hardly look purple at all now, just bright white crowding spots dancing on your eyes. At least from a distance they look like flowers; close up, you can see that they're not quite right. Each fat petal sticks out separately from the hairy, sappy stalk; they haven't quite come together into a proper flower.

"What are they called, these flowers?"

He says some fancy name, *Lapidarium* something. "Most people call them a winsome blue, or a welcome blue."

"Blue? They're not *blue*! That up *there*'s blue! These are white, little bit purple."

"Ah, yeah. But blue's in the eye of the beholder, you'll find. Like a lotta things."

"Like beauty, you mean?" It sounds funny for me to say a word like "beauty"—even funnier to say it out here, with this guy. Like Mrs. Allan saying "gorgeous."

"Yairs, that, too."

"Don't you like them?"

He looks at me, at the field of blues, back to me. "Liking doesn't come into it, exactly, liking or not liking."

And he pours himself more milky tea from the thermos. I listen to him sip, to his old throat swallowing. The silence seems to be thicker now, the insect noises getting higher and farther away. I dip and turn my head, because it seems to me that there's a different noise happening, almost too low to hear, a kind of throbbing, very faint. Maybe I'm hearing my own blood out here, my own heartbeat, in the quiet.

A sharp-edged shadow moves across the sun and stops

on the field of winsome blues. My mouth drops open and I look to Quaid.

He gets up with a long grunt, takes his tea mug out into the open and looks up. "Well, I'll be a monkey's uncle."

I run out to him. There's something in the air that's like the bottom of a big black iron. It's as long as a bus, wide as two buses here at the back end. It hovers over the field, kind of nosing around. When it moves, it makes the throbbing noise; when it stops, the throbbing fades. Bit by bit it comes lower and lower and turns right around so that it's pointed towards the shed.

"What is it?" I whisper.

Quaid drains his tea mug. "It must be their nonsense downtown."

"What, these are the *gods*?"

"Well, the . . ." He squints up at the giant floating iron. "Let's just wait and see, shall we?"

I take a deep breath. Okay. I'll start freaking when *he* starts.

The iron thing locks into position and comes down real careful. The tip of its beak is about a metre from Quaid's boot toe. He shakes the tea dregs onto the ground behind him. The iron thing nuzzles the dry grass, and settles there.

Two trickles come out of the tip of the beak, like steam that doesn't float away. They grow to the size of children, waist-high to Quaid. And they kind of *boil*. They look like these caterpillars I saw once on a nature program that were being all eaten up inside by these wormy parasite things, so that they were really just sacks of writhing maggots.

One of the things speaks, in a chittering voice that makes the maggots writhe faster. "Thanking you for welcome. Most appropriately beautiful." They bow towards the crop.

Quaid eyes the flowers, too, then gives the creatures a nod. "A pleasure. Can I offer you a cuppa tea, maybe?"

The two things chitter doubtfully at each other, swaying on their stalks.

"Or something to eat? Bit of sausage? Bit of pickle?"

They come to a decision. "Thanking, thanking. Already are eaten."

"Come a long way, have you?" says Quaid.

They put what seem to be their head ends together to giggle. Then they bend their joined heads towards us, still giggling, and—well, they blow *my* mind. It isn't so much where they come from, which is about what you'd expect of caterpillar-land—lots of juicy food and wriggling and cocoon-weaving—so much as the hugeness between that place and this one, the fact of Earth being so tiny and so almost-lost among all the other places they've been, and the empty distance—empty even of blackness, empty even of a lonely whistling wind—between us and everything else. My brain feels like a giant emptied eggshell, with just the few slimy strands that are me, that are Earth-stuff, twanging stupidly in all that space.

"Ah," says Quaid. He rocks onto his heels and pushes his free hand into his work-pants pocket. "You planning on staying long?"

"Already we late, having to return. But our greeting. Purse of welcome? Bring when you come, him." One of the little maggots bursts out of the caterpillar-skin and falls to the grass, wagging. "Must thanking and go. Again, very fine flag you grown. Most joyous and delightful."

"Lovely flag," agrees the other. "Be going and goodbye, planetaries."

"'bye, then," says Quaid.

The two creatures shrivel back into the tip of the iron. It throbs, and goes straight up in a quick, nifty spiral into the blue, leaving no smoke or noise, not even flattened grass.

The insects start up shrilling all around us. The breeze gently knocks at us, and the flower stalks squeak and rustle.

"So you *knew* they'd come here, all the time?" I say wonderingly.

"Hadn't a clue." Quaid pokes at the maggot with his toe.

I kneel on the grass and have a look at it. It's not moving anymore, and it's gone all brown and dead-looking, like a dried-up seed-pod. I pick it up—it's heavy, and it rattles. And it *is* a pod—a row of slots has opened along one side of it, and inside each slot a pale, fat disc is loosely trapped, streaked with the same pinky-mauve as the very edge of a winsome-blue petal. I touch one of the discs; it's smooth and waxy, like a fresh-peeled bean.

"A purse of welcome," says Quaid. "Some kind of space money." He looks up at the empty sky, then goes under the shelter and starts lining flower boxes.

I carry the maggot-purse in after him. "Shouldn't we tell someone?"

He bends to put boxes on the lower shelf of the trolley. "Hm? Like who, d'you reckon?"

"The police? The newspapers? At least those people down the valley."

Quaid's eyebrows shoot up.

"Don't you want to tell 'em they missed out?" I say.

"Reckon they'd be pretty browned orf, most of 'em." He starts lining flower boxes with tissue.

"Yeah, *wouldn't* they!"

"And the ones that weren't . . . well, it'd be the Prophet Quaid this and the Holy Relic Space Money that—"

"Yeah! Great, hey? I wouldn't mind being the Prophet Eleanor. Can I have this, if you're not going to use it?" I say, turning the purse over in my hands.

He doesn't answer. He's looking at me, chuckling quietly through his nose, his mouth twitching with things he could say.

Finally, "By all means," he says, "you keep the purse, Eleanor." And he pulls his flower trolley out towards the crop.

I hold the purse and turn one of the waxy discs in its slot. It's mine. I could walk up to the road right this minute, hitch a ride to the showground, worm my way through the crowd to a microphone. Whatever I said, they'd do it; they're gathered together all ready to be told, to get their instructions from the gods. They'd *want* me to come—remember Mrs. Allan's crumpling face? *It's people's most heartfelt beliefs!*

I look up from the purse. Quaid's already nearly halfway down his row, seeming to move slowly but cutting faster than I ever will. The sunlight's blinding on his bent back, on the crowding spots of the flowers.

Sigh. I put the purse down in the shade, with a milk crate over it so it won't get stepped on. I go to my trolley and line all the boxes, and unhook my knife from the wall. And I trundle out into the sunlight, and get on with my work.

| | | |

WEALTH

"Absolutely not." I turned on my heel.

Lar grabbed my arm. I took pleasure in snatching it out of his grasp; it's not often an Ord can show open contempt for a Leet. I stalked away through the crowd of students.

He came hurrying after me, steadying the great braided pile of his hair. In the Leet tongue, the word for *hair* is the same as the word for *wealth*, and Lar was *wealthy*—but not as wealthy as he wanted to be, not as wealthy as he wanted me to make him.

"I can *pay* you," he said.

"That should make a difference?"

"I can pay you a *lot*."

"Too bad, Lar. Some of us aren't for sale."

"But you're the *best*!"

His despair made me smile. It was the first time a nubile Leet had tried to bribe me to augment him—I couldn't help but feel proud. My own head, shorn like most Ords', was high and my step was light as I swept out the college gate. My work must be getting good circulation, I must be becoming a name worth dropping. I would share this with Purl as soon as I got to the workshop.

But Purl was waiting for me. She came hurrying up the laneway to meet me, her face tight with controlled emotions. She caught me by the shoulders. "They have taken Chirrup again."

I swallowed a curse. "What for?"

"For throwing flour on glory-day. At the procession. A *nothing* charge, a mere nuisance—"

"He is under the Wall?"

She nodded, fiercely blinking back tears. "In a Protocol cell."

"I will go there. Directly." I thrust my book-satchel into her arms.

She could not disguise her relief. "Good girl! You know I would go myself, if I were allowed there—"

"Yes, I know."

"Give him my love!" she cried after me.

Yes, well . . .

My annoyance sped me through the busy market square. My grandmother's love had always been divided unequally between my brother and me. For all my hard work, for all the skill I put to use in Purl's augmentation shop, for all my steady fulfilment of my obligations to her, I could never strike the spark in her eye that Chirrup could, greeting her nonchalantly as he left the house, snatching his breakfast off my plate on the way. Purl complained about the bronze-coin I cost her with each season's college-fee, but Chirrup could wander, free of occupation, all day, bringing in no coin yet availing himself of bed and board in her house, and not a sour word would she utter. And the lengths she'd gone to, to scrape together the *twenty gilden* his last trip to the Wall had cost her! And did he do anything to repay her, besides come home and lift her off her feet, and let her cover his face with kisses? And yet she had seemed entirely content with that.

They brought Chirrup up to the visiting cell. He grunted when he saw me. I guess he expected a co-conspirator, to be gleeful with, or maybe that quadroon-girl I'd seen him with, the one in the leathers.

"Purl sends her love," I said flatly.

"Mph. She send any money?"

"They've set a price on you, then?"

"Hmm." He sniffed. I could read this boy like a book;

he was a little frightened of the amount, yet impressed with himself, itching to tell.

"Twenty, same as last time?" I tried to sound as if I didn't care one way or another. "Throwing flour isn't as bad as sloganing a wall, but for a second misdeed—"

"Sixty," he said.

I gaped.

"*Because* of last time." A sort of glum pride shaped his face.

"But Purl can never pay—"

"I know that—"

"I know you know," I snapped back. "It's the surprise talking."

He snorted. "You would make a crap rebel."

"Who'd *want* to be a rebel?" I rang one of the bars between us with a knuckle. "Petty vandals and jail worms, the lot of you. Daubing walls, setting fart-bombs—it's all so much *playing*. Being a rebel used to mean something, but who could take you seriously these days?"

He gave an irritatingly patient sigh. "You don't know anything."

"I know there's a grandmother somewhere eating her heart out over your carry-on; I know that much."

He rolled his eyes. "And if it weren't for Leets I'd have a mother and father, too. Get Purl to tell you *that* story, dolling girl, fawner on our oppressors."

"I don't *fawn*!"

"Prettying up pet tamsins all day—you call that taking a stand for the Ord Nation, do you?" he said with a smirk.

"I call it earning my keep. *Someone* has to repay Purl for the food we eat and the roof over our heads. *This* looks like a Leet roof to me." I waved at the arched brick ceiling of the cell.

"Wrong!" he crowed. "This is Ord work, built before colony times. Pick up a history book some time."

I gripped the bars between us as if *I* were the prisoner. "I know *my* history," I said in a low voice. "I share all my working hours with our grandmother, remember? She should be a Wise One, honoured, with an easy life. Instead, she has to pickle her hands in live-water every day, slaving for noble toy-people. Ord history is written in the bend of Purl's back, in the lines on her face, if you'd only look. And *you*, you do nothing more than worsen that woman's pain. You can spout all the rebel preachery you like, but I can smell your breath, the fancy onioned Leet food on it. At least I have never stunk like you. And many more of their meals you'll be eating, while Purl breaks law and friendship buying you out of here. I hope you're pleased."

"It's her choice," he said smugly. And he stood there smiling and shrugging at me, handsome and stupid as ever. He was lucky the bars were there, I tell you, or I would have clawed his pretty green eyes out with my bare hands.

| | | |

I walked slowly back across the square. Most of the stallholders were packing and leaving, and the cries of the last fresh-goods vendors had an evening echo, bell-like and tragic, quite different from their businesslike daytime clamour. Sixty gilden. Sixty! I remembered Purl counting out the twenty last spring. *I have never seen this much money in my life*, I had thought then, *and I may never again.*

Sixty was mad. Sixty was impossible; the law knew that. Sixty meant they wanted him off the streets. Which was ridiculous. So he was a rebel—what did rebels ever do? They set off smoke-bombs, they scribbled slogans on walls, they fomented crazy rumours about seizing power and scouring Leets from the land. They were a shadow of their former force, of which our parents had been part. Didn't the law know that? Hadn't Leet law itself taken all our power away, right by right, rebel by rebel?

"He's fine," I told Purl, back at the workshop. "Well fed. They haven't set a price on him yet." It was easier to lie than to see her face fall, hear her weep and wail. I wanted a rest from having Chirrup on my brain, from pretending to care whether he lived or died. And there was no other way for her to find out—Purl and all her friends were smudged and smeared with old rebel connections themselves, and could not go near the Wall.

I put on an apron and settled to my work. Chirrup might sneer at it, might rightly condemn it as yet another bowing to Leets' will, but I loved it, for its delicacy and beauty, and for the repetitiveness that emptied my head of thoughts of family, of politics, of anything at all. The tamsin's pelt rose and fell under my fingers as I brightened and thickened its coat, adding wealth strand by silky new strand. I was *good* at this; even Purl couldn't have told the new hairs from the old.

This was a fine, fine beast I was working on, from deep within the Keys, so highly strung that they'd had to drug it and bring it in on its tasselled cushion. Its claws were beaten metal, its eye-rims tattooed black just like a Leet's. They were so stupidly competitive, Leets. The money they poured into these lap-beasts!

But I can pay you! Lar's voice cried out in my memory, so sudden that I almost set a hair awry.

"You're all right, Rill?" said Purl sharply behind me. She knew what wealth lay under my hands.

"I'm fine." I took a breath and tried not to concentrate too hard, or I'd start setting the hairs in rows, instead of properly randomly.

I can pay you a lot!

I held steady this time, but all my skin was prickling. What was "a lot" of money, for a Leet? To be sure, it would make sixty gilden look like loose change. But it would be some embarrassing amount, a problem to hide. And all the equipment I'd have to "borrow" from the workshop to grow the hair, without anyone noticing— crazy! And then, how could I *move* such a weight of wealth? Human wealth was long—it was no use unless it brushed the floor—and it would die without live-water. I would have to smuggle Lar *in*—But why was I even *thinking* this way?—

"Your mind is elsewhere, girl." Purl wished she could control that part of me, too.

"Yes, grandmother." I paused to ease the tension in my shoulders. "I'm thinking about Chirrup."

"Ah." As I bent over the work again she placed a hand on my back, and for a few moments I basked in the true sympathy my false virtue had bought me, before the sadness of it seeped through to me.

I lifted another comb of tamsin wealth from the cask beside me. Taking bribes, breaking law to help some Leet advance her child—I shook my head. As if I would ever waste my skills like that. As if I would so compromise myself.

But in the middle of that night, a voice woke me—my

own this time, not Lar's. I opened my eyes on the darkness, and the voice said, *A boy-head is not so different from a tamsin-head . . . is it?*

| | | |

Leets are supposed to learn alongside us up to marrying age, so that they develop the touch for dealing with commoners. But of course, except for the real goody-goodies, they never come near us, not to converse, not to pass time. So it was in the morning rush, when Ord and Leet mingled on the college paths and in the corridors, that I veered through the crowd to Lar's elbow and said calmly, "I have been giving it some thought, what you proposed."

He drew back from me, blinking a flash of delight from his eyes. Then he leaned forward with unnervingly obvious eagerness. "My house, tonight."

"Are you sure you wouldn't like to come to *my* house?" I said in the same hushed, excited tone, just to watch his blank confusion. Then I rescued him. "Don't worry. I'll be there at sunset." Sourly I enjoyed the relief on his face before I let the crowd sweep me away from him.

| | | |

I had fully expected not to be admitted to Lar's house, so I felt shaky and strange to be barefoot inside, moving down a polished red-rock hall between windows full of darkening garden, following a door-servant all dolled into glistering armour, his Ord hair sleekened to a red-gold cap. He was quite a spectacle in himself; I would have liked some time to examine him.

But greater wonders called me. The hall gave onto a bedroom, bright as a cloth-merchant's stall with hangings and rugs. Lar was there, arranged on a dais among plump embroidered cushions, his wealth flowing out from his head in rivers of shining gold.

"Ah, Rill!" His voice was charmed and charming; then it flattened out—"Very well"—as he dismissed the door-man. As soon as we were alone his face sagged. But even in front of humble old me he could not help himself preening, little tossings of the head, little strokings of the hair. The hours he must spend tending all that wealth! Not to mention carting it around with him, like potatoes, like animal feed.

"You'll do it, then," he said, as if he'd never had any doubt of it.

"For a price."

His mouth turned into a righteous little purse. "My mother said you would be greedy. She said to tell you to remember that this could bring more money later, from others."

"Well, you can tell your mother I'm doing this just the once, and only because family happenings drive me to it."

"Really?" Lar gave me an eager, expectant look, but I was not going to widen his eyes any further with tales of rebels and jails. He sighed. "How much, then?"

I reached for the number that had kept me awake last night, a number I could not quite believe, a rumour-number, a fantastical number. "A round thousand," I said.

His face went pale. "We are not High Leet, you know."

"But I will make you High. As you said, I am the best."

Footsteps sounded outside, and someone came into the room behind me. I stood motionless, staring at the far wall-hanging—a flower maze, typically overwrought.

"She wants a thousand," Lar said to the newcomer.

There was a short silence, then the rustle of robes as Lar's mother walked slowly around me, at a good distance—so as not to contaminate herself, no doubt.

She turned to face me. "It's Rill, is it?"

I was supposed to bow; instead, I looked her in the eye. "Yes."

That nettled her. "I have not seen your work, nor heard of it, though Lar tells me others think well of you."

Normally I would not speak unless she questioned me. But, "Every lap-beast in this part of the Keys has something of my work in it. Your own tamsin, Therial, is all mine. And your older son's beast."

"Mink?" Lar sat forward excitedly. "You augmented her?" he asked, in spite of his mother's signal to be silent.

"Finest watering. Very difficult on an opal tamsin."

"But she's gorgeous!—"

"Lar, be quiet."

He flounced back against his satiny cushions.

"My son has no gifts but his looks," said his mother. She herself was beautiful enough, although she had the kind of eye-rims that will not take a tattoo. Several attempts had been made, but instead of forming clear, dark lines the ink had spread into smudgy shadows. "Fortunately, there is a fashion for trophy husbands among High Leet, particularly among older women who have nothing left to prove. He is pretty enough, but he has no advantages other than the one you will give him. You understand what hangs on this?"

"All your family's fortunes, ma'am."

She lifted a heavily jewelled index finger at me. "And yours, too. Remember that."

"I am certain I will lose neither."

She scrutinised me for a long moment. "What else will you need?"

"A three-day pass, two for the work, one for the setting, the day before the weighing."

"The day before?" said Lar doubtfully. "Don't you need to leave time for me to heal?"

"Only if I'm going to botch the job, which I'm not."

Lar's mother took a jar of live-water out of her belt-purse and went to the dais. "Hold still." She took her time choosing three good strands of her son's wealth. Lar winced as she plucked them from his scalp. She wound them around her fingers and slipped the golden loop into the jar. No fuss, no haggling. I could hardly believe my luck.

| | | | |

The way home took me through the Vines district. I was so full-headed, reliving my appointment at Lar's house, that I hardly noticed how dark it was, how the street-lamps were choked with creepers, how few traders and how many night-people were abroad in the narrow streets.

In a lane lined with rag-trade houses, a hooded figure rose from the shadow of a doorway and stood in my path. "Miss, miss," it said and held out its hand—a young, strong hand, at which I stared suspiciously.

Other hands seized me from behind. *And the shoulders are too broad,* I thought, as a gag-cloth choked off my cry. *And there was something faked in his voice.* But it was laughably too late by then.

They forced me through the doorway into a long, dark hall smelling of cheap dye and ant mould. They pushed me to the end of it, up some flimsy stairs and into a small room, lit brightly with pressure lamps, their bases filthy but their glass invisibly clean.

A handsome Ord faced us over a table piled with maps, his red hair flaring to his broad, bare shoulders. The "beggar" cut the braid of my belt-purse and took it to him, and murmured in his ear. The man emptied the purse onto the table, straight away picked up the live-water jar and shot me an amused glance. He waved the murmurer away, and made a sign to the others. They took off my gag, but left my hands bound behind me.

"You must be Rill, sister of our man Chirrup." He stood and came around the table, his gaze on the jar in his hand.

"And you are the rebel Rustle," I said, surprised and trying not to show it. I'd always imagined some mean little skulking thug, not this tall, bright-eyed strongman. *Chirrup should've warned me*, I thought, unfairly.

"How is your brother, then?" said Rustle, without the trace of sarcasm I would've used.

"Well enough."

He turned the jar in his long, scarred fingers. "I would say—well, it could be anything between fifty-five and eighty gilden they have set on him, hm? To drive you to this?"

I said nothing.

He put down the jar and pushed his hands into his pockets. His pants were the old combat style, worn by a lot of Ords for manual labour—or for rebel show. Rustle's were almost rags; I could imagine Chirrup drooling at the sight of them. "You have to be cool-headed in this business. Your brother is not, although he tries hard, I'll grant you. We had a big job lined up for when he'd proven his mettle, but then glory-day came along, and he couldn't contain himself." Rustle's smile was growing in warmth. His skin was thickly freckled; on his cheeks the freckles had joined together in patches of oddly Leet-looking colour, but he had green Ord eyes. He could have been brother to my brother. A brother with more than half a brain; wouldn't that have been interesting? "How do *you* feel about losing your parents to the colonists, Miss Rill?"

"Nothing," I said. "I hardly remember them—and Chirrup was a babe in arms. It happened to lots of people. And what's the point? No one can get them back."

Someone spat on the floor behind me. "Fatalist."

"Excellent," said Rustle. "However. Chirrup is no use to us under the Wall, is he?"

"Pay his way out, then, and save me the work."

Rustle gave a little laugh, then came close to me and smiled down into my eyes. "But all my sources tell me you *enjoy* working," he said softly. I kept my face stubborn and did not drop my gaze modestly as I was tempted to do. "That you are *devoted*. Not to mention highly skilled."

He looked down on me a moment longer, then turned away—I was relieved and disappointed both. He went to the desk and idly picked up the jar again. "I hope Lar's mother is paying you well. I wouldn't ask under a thousand if I were you." He glanced sidelong at me. I kept my face as blank as I could. This was no guesswork he was doing; the man had had me followed! I didn't know rebels could keep such a close eye on things.

He laughed again. "Good," he said. "Good, because we can't pay you anything. I'd love to—as I said, it's a big job we wanted Chirrup to do for us. I'd love to be able to toss gilden around like bronze-coin, a head-price here, a gift there; I'd love to be able to buy my way to victory the way Lar's mother can. But that's our whole point, isn't it? Lar's mother has the money, and rebel Rustle doesn't. I can't reach into my purse for help; I must reach into my brain. I can't buy you, and I don't have time to talk you around. All I can do is remind you—your guild has laws against the augmenting of noble wealth. Do I need to say any more?"

I sighed. "No."

"Hm. You're smarter than your brother. But you probably know that."

"Flatterer. What must I do?"

He sat behind the desk again. All pretence and charm dropped away from his face, and his voice. Instantly I liked him better, until I heard what he was saying. "You'll ask for a Key, an extra day's pass, and a set of robes for the weighing-day ceremony. You want to see your work for what it is, tell them, for what it wins. Otherwise, you say, the deal is off. I will hold this wealth as surety."

"No." I stepped forward. Someone jerked me back. Lar's looped hairs gleamed at me, turning in the liquid. "Why should I go to a weighing?"

"You'll take something in for me, into the weigh-hall."

"I won't throw flour or paint! I won't get arrested! It'd kill my grandmother—"

"There'll be no throwing anything." He watched me calm down—my hard breathing was the only sound in the room. "Tell Lar tomorrow. Be firm; insist that this is part of your fee. Tomorrow night you may have your jar back, the night after if the boy needs to check with his mother. Don't worry, you'll get what you ask; the mother is desperate." He looked past me. "Let her go."

They untied my hands. I glanced behind me: three ruffians, one a gap-toothed girl, all in some kind of leatherwear, all with that pretentious rebel hair. They stood aside from the door, and the girl mock-obsequiously bowed and waved me towards it.

I took a last uncertain look at Rustle, at his bright, level stare. Then I left, trying not to scuttle, keeping as straight a back as I could.

| | | |

"What kind of torture is this?" cried Purl, drumming her fists on the kitchen table. "Why keep us all waiting? Don't they want their money? How am I to find it without knowing how much to find?"

"It will probably be twenty gilden, like last time," I said, stirring the grains of my supper in the warming thin-milk. "Possibly less—flour-throwing is a lesser deed than writing slogans."

"Oh, it will be more. He has shown himself a rebel; they will want forty at least. I should start hunting for that forty."

"I tell you, Grandmother, wait. Don't go finding lawless ways to money you might not even need."

"Not *need*? Fool girl, is he such a grand rebel that they will not set a head-price? You know nothing of these things, with your face in books and tamsin-fur all day."

I nodded and stirred. I was more tired than I had ever been in my life. Which was why I misjudged the tone of my next remark.

"You're right—what would I know?" Something of all

the many things I *did* know slipped out among the words.

Purl was up from the table and at me. She grabbed my chin, her claws in my cheeks, and roughly pulled my face around to read it. "They've set it, haven't they? Don't lie to me. How much? How much!"

"They haven't," I said feebly. Her heart was frighteningly visible in her face, full of fear and rage.

She slapped me. The spoon flipped out of the grain-pan and trailed a spiral of milk through the air. I didn't hear the clatter of its landing under Purl's screaming. "How much, cruel girl? Tell me or I will kill you with these very hands!"

"Uh . . . hundred," I said, holding my cheek. Well, I couldn't keep pretending, could I? Not for all the weeks it would take me to do this work for Lar. And a hundred she would despair of ever finding, whereas she might still make a fool of herself trying for sixty.

She fell back from me, fell silent. Her face was so grey and dread-full, I thought she would die of it. She turned from me; she shrank into herself; she all but crawled away upstairs.

Shaking, I bent to pick up the spoon. My face stung, and my jaw felt bruised where she'd grabbed me. With a cloth I slowly wiped the thin-milk off the spoon, and off the floor all the way back to the stove. I hated her, I hated them all, Lar and his greedy mother, Rustle and his ruffians, stupid Chirrup and whatever stupid Leet-servant had arrested him. *Let* the deal be off; why should I lift a finger for any of them? I would tell Lar I'd had an attack of conscience; Rustle could keep the jar—or hand it in, for all I cared. What could he prove, after all? And the mother could find some other augmenter, some greedy second best; and me, I would go back to tamsin-prettying.

Let Chirrup rot, let Rustle flatter someone else, let Purl—

I started to stir again.

Purl, greying and shrinking and shuffling away . . .

A hateful scene played itself out behind my eyes: Chirrup coming home last time. I was behind him, the empty money-sack in my hand. I saw Purl rise and fly across the room to him; I saw her face. I'd brought her the light of her life.

A little sobbing breath came out of me. I wiped my eyes and nose on my sleeve, banged a bowl down on the table and poured in the not-quite-cooked slop. I turned off the hissing stove, flung myself down and began to eat.

| | | |

"So, are you in love with her?" I suppressed a yawn and leaned on Lar's balcony railing.

Light was sinking out of the sky, pink fading to mauve and then to blue. The lightless Vines gaped below; along the far promenade the path-lamps buzzed. I wished I was walking there, listening to sea-sounds. A nubile Leet is a seriously dull companion, interested only in hairstyles and marriage prospects.

Lar made an impatient sound. "I've just got to get matched, that's all. This summer, or my mother will desert me. And the girl's wealthy. Everyone wants her."

"What if you don't get matched with her?" Ha! Hadn't he heard his mother? His best chance was with some old scandal-mongress with a lot of money to throw at a pretty-boy. But who could blame him for fantasising?

"Oh, someone lesser will do. That girl of Heddering's is all right. Felice is all right. Either of those."

"And if they fall through?"

He put his hands to his face. "Oh, then we're getting pretty desperate. Oath, maybe? Jenna's cousin? At *least*!" Now he looked worried.

"You aim pretty high," I said.

"If I can just up my wealth a bit . . ."

"It already looks a little upped, to me."

"Beast-hair. Dead padding."

"Good boy."

He looked at me. "Sometimes I think you Ords have it pretty good."

Oh, don't start. "Well, there's no existence quite as meaningful as one spent augmenting lap pets, I tell you. Eat your heart out, pretty man."

"But it doesn't *matter* with whom you match. You can just *decide*, two of you together. You don't have this awful *event*, where you get held up in public and gawped at by jealous everyone."

"Ah no, we are just held down, daily, while everyone looks away." This was Chirrup-talk, just to be annoying. But the bitterness in my voice was truly felt, I realised—Lar's stupidity in the midst of this dolled house was doing something to me.

He sent me an uneasy glance and fiddled with one of the many bows of his snood. "Yes, well . . . that's not exactly *my* doing—"

I recognised his mother's quick footsteps in the corridor—no servant ever walked that fast.

"Here," she said, coming straight to me as if I were the only person in the room. She thrust the cloth-wrapped parcel of robes at me. "I have slipped the pass and Key in the pocket. If you are stopped and searched, you are on your way to Patter's laundry to have these cleaned, on errand for me. Feign surprise that the things are there and offer to return them to me at once. Do you understand?"

"Of course." I was full of confidence. Rustle had returned me my jar a week ago and I had already grown a good swag of wealth. The more nervous Lar and his mother grew, the more serene I felt.

"Very well. Get home and hide it, then. I will send Lar to you on the day, as we arranged."

And she hustled me out of the room, not giving me a chance to make farewells to Lar, as if he no more required them than any other piece of fancy furniture in the room.

| | | |

Every day at breakfast Purl was grey-faced and silent, punishing *me* for Chirrup's foolishness.

"I'll go and see him again this afternoon, if you want," I said.

She made a noise in her throat and kept staring up at the window.

"I can take him any message you like. Or clambroth, if you make it. He loves that."

She tore a piece of bread from the chunk on her plate, and chewed it hard, her eyes filling. The tears spilled and fell to the table. She chewed on, her gaze fixed on the window, her face angry, even with the tears running down it.

| | | |

"You'll carry a bouquet and a gift," said Rustle. "Are you going augmented yourself?"

I shook my head. "I'll wear a taped snood with ear-locks sewn in. I've already made it." I'd made it just so he would give me that look, the appraising, set-back-on-his-heels one. Pleasure and disgust at myself surged equally strong in me.

"And the wealth increases, does it?"

"Like a pond of golden-eel." In fact, I'd had no small difficulty hiding all the new wealth, swirling golden in its live-water. I'd had to lay my bed-plank across cask-tops to make room for it all. For a change, I was glad I was an only daughter, with a room of my own.

"And all else is well?" I could almost believe Rustle was seeing *me* rather than a cogwheel in his nuisance-machine.

"Why yes, unless you count Purl's dying of grief as mattering much."

There was some kindness in his smile. "While Chirrup lives, she will live. It's a tough old bird, that bird Hope."

"Hmph. Maybe. I don't see the harm in telling her our plan, myself."

"Which does not mean there is none." He reached across the weighing-hall map, touched my arm and looked into my eyes. My pulse sprang erratic at his touch. "Take my word, Rill. I know where danger is."

I cleared my throat. "So what will be in the gift?" I said while I had him. "A smell, an itch? Indelible paint?"

He looked blank for a moment, then smiled a smile to disguise some other expression. "You need not know," he said. "You need not worry your head." And his gaze moved over my bare scalp for a moment before reading in my eyes whether he needed to go on.

"No, I've never thought of growing it," I said bluntly.

Which was true enough—it had occurred to me I'd make a better rebel disguised as a neat, poll-headed, down-trodden Ord. But I wasn't going to tell him that; I had some pride. I wanted him to ask me. He could force me to do this first job, but he'd have to properly ask me for anything further.

He didn't. "Pity," he said, so breathily, so airily, I hardly trusted myself to have heard it. I felt a great hollowness between us, as if we were regarding each other across a deep, wide chasm, the world's noise making it impossible to speak. And Rustle got up from the table and was going to the door, which he would open and stand beside as he always did, to show me our meetings were over.

| | | |

"Four days?" Purl thrust the card from her, then snatched it back to glare at it.

"As you see, Grandmother," I said.

"Are you mad? Who is this? A high doctor! What in all the red-headed blazing heavens is this?"

"A friend got me in to him."

"A friend? With whom have you been mixing?"

"Why do you send me to that college, then?"

"For *appearances*, fool-girl. What is this?"

"I want the full four days solitary, for my bleeding and all the ceremony around it."

"Bleeding and ceremony? Now? When all the high-born want their laps full of tamsins at the weighing?"

"Am I not entitled, whenever?"

"Well, *entitled* is one thing. But whoever *takes* those four days?"

"People who need them, maybe."

She looked up at me, hearing the strain in my voice that came from lying but could be read as something else.

"You have been very strange."

"Maybe I have."

"Have you been with a man or something?"

"No!"

"Are you in lust?"

"No! Stop it!"

She watched my long blushing. She took a deep breath in through her nose and released it out her mouth. She tucked the pass-card into her sleeve.

"Take the four days—why should I care? But don't think you'll get it every month."

"I don't. I won't. Just this once." And I slouched away.

| | | |

Two days I clambered about my room, which was more cask room than sleeping room now. I used the middle-day, when Purl was at the workshop, to do the heavy cask moving and emptying and water carting. Mornings and evenings were for selection.

Boy-hair was so straight and coarse and round, so different from tamsins' ∞-profiled strands, which sometimes split down the middle, whole batches at a time ruined. At first I thought there were no discards, each strand looked so robust and shining.

But after a while of working, my eye began to discern differences. I could just give Lar *more* wealth, or I could give him, by taking some care, *spectacular* wealth in degree of shine, in strength and straightness. It was bulk he wanted, but I would not give him more of what he already had; I would give him bulk that screamed richesse, that blinded the Leets' eyes when the weighing-room lamps hit it. I worked my own eyes and my fingers red and sore those two days—and nights I gave, too, as much as I could without falling asleep into the selection-tub.

Late the second night I had it all as I needed, the wealth draped in a great shining semicircle from the cask onto sheets on the floor, the instruments in their boiling-cases, several sets for safety. All the other casks were put back behind the shop; all the discarded wealth was drained and sold, discreetly, to a dealer in the Vines, one with no connection to our usual buyer of tamsin-wealth. And I sat for several minutes, my hands empty, my eyes full of wealth-glister, in a state of bewilderment at myself, before my practical brain sent me to bed.

| | | |

"Oh, my wealth!" gasped Lar when he came in next morning. "That's it? That's mine?"

"Sit down." I was tired, I was fed up looking at the stuff. I wanted to get started so that I could get done.

He went and bent over the cask. "But it's fantastic! This is from *my* wealth?"

"Sit down. We must get started."

I tell you, I earned my money and more in just that day. And not only in the setting of that great crop of wealth in Master Lar's scalp.

"You must not cry," I said. "You will ruin your eyes for tomorrow."

"But it so hurts! With every hair! Ow!" And he pulled away from me so that the hair I had just set came uprooted, and there was a bead of blood.

We came to an agreement; he would not cry or move if, after every seven hairs, I paused for him to complain and recover. And apart from a couple of stormy moments, he held good. He had to; we had only one day and night, and there was enormous effort in this, despite the ease of setting such big-toy hair. Just keeping the long hair free of tangles as I worked necessitated so much careful combing, so much more than a tamsin's!

I was soon thoroughly sick of Lar's hard golden-brown scalp and the whimpering coming from underneath it. It wasn't until evening, when we stopped our second time for food and drink, that the excitement took me, seeing the way the old hair was puffed out by the new. The effects of my two days' careful selection took fire in the dim light.

"You'll love it!" I whispered, for Purl was home from work and moving about downstairs by then. "Your mother will be so happy!"

Lar chewed and looked at me sidelong. "It had better work," he almost snarled. He looked exhausted, but there was nothing a little sleep, a little paint could not correct.

Deep in the night, we finished. He would not let me comb it all straight. "Just put it in a bag loose. I can't stand this any longer." So I did, not even knowing how to plait or order such long hair; I straightened it out as best I could, the armfuls of it, and put it in a loose knot in a makeshift snood of sheeting.

"Get me out of here." He stood up and scraped his chair back.

"Ssh! You'll wake my grandmother."

"Screw your grandmother."

"My, my—somebody's a little tetchy."

Lar gave me a savage look and held out the waist-bands of the snood for me to tie.

It was an hour beyond midnight. We stood in silence on the doorstep until our eyes shed the golden light of my room, then hurried to Modern Square, where Lar's house equipage waited. His mother burst from the carriage door as we crossed the square. "The volume is good," she said in a hard voice.

"Oh, it's so *heavy*!" whined Lar. "Heavier than the padding."

"Relish it, boy." She reached up and pulled back the sheet. My work on the hairline, interspersing Lar's thinner, duller hair with the very best of the new-grown strands, showed even in the moonlight—*fat* growth of gleaming wealth.

"Look at that! Not a mark or a blood-bead to be seen. This is good work, honest girl!" She grinned so evilly at me, I could not take it for a compliment. "I will recommend you. Do you want that? This could be profitable business for you."

"If you see fit," I said. Formality is so handy, for filling a gaping mouth.

She laughed some more, stroking her son's forehead. Then, "Into the car," she snapped.

As Lar hauled himself and his new wealth away, she handed me a big pocket of coin. "Here is half, in gilden. The bronze is in a pack in the carriage—too heavy for any but an Ordinary."

When I had shouldered it, she pulled back from fussing Lar into the car, and she *kissed* me! "Bless you," she said. "You have made history tonight." Then she climbed up, and the carriage drew away.

I struggled home and stuffed the bronze-pack into my clothes-chest, then emptied the gilden onto my bed and counted them, twice. One hundred gilden, five times over. I shook my head over it, I laughed in awe. Why had I done this? I would *absolutely not* do it, I had said to Lar— but then I had wavered, and Rustle had trapped me so that I could not waver *back*, and now it was done, all but Rustle's little job, after which I would be my own person again. And stronger for having wavered this once, and found out what it led to.

I'd be sensible, distance myself from all that rebel nonsense, hang onto the money, finish college, set myself up in a slow and modest-looking way. One of those specialty workshops between the Vines and the Keys, the ones with only a discreet name-board beside the door— one of those was mine, lying before me in the form of coin. It would be so *easy* now! I had seen the appeal of the lawless life—but I was stopping right here, of course. Purl, Chirrup, Rustle, Lar, and his mother—what did I owe any of them? I didn't truly care for Rustle's cause, and I wasn't going to join him just for the sake of belonging somewhere. Whatever I felt when I was near him, I wouldn't let him turn my head. I would be strong, and lone, and rich, and keep quiet about it, keep my mouth shut and my nose clean, so I would.

And with a huge yawn, I began stashing away my new wealth.

| | | |

I took twenty in gilden and the rest in bronze, so as not to arouse suspicion. I went early, before even the market people were abroad, when there was no colour in the world, only first light like grey sand swimming in the air.

At the Wall they kept me waiting, as if they couldn't bring themselves to touch my money. I sat there with the sack between my feet, while the jailers had long, idle conversations, casting me blank looks every now and again. I concentrated on not sighing or moving, not showing any irritation that would invite them to delay me longer.

"Put your penalty on that table," a guard finally said to me. "And you may as well go through."

More waiting in another room. I began to worry about the time this was taking. I had things to do. I had a bag full of weigh-clothes to get into.

Finally I heard them pour out the money and count through it, the musical chinking of the heavy gilden and the workaday rattle of the bronze. And then sooner than I expected, Chirrup came to the door.

He gave a showy yawn. "What kind of hour is this to get a man out of bed?"

"Go home and make Purl some breakfast," I said, getting up off the cold stone bench and slinging my bag onto my shoulder.

"Why, what did she have to do?"

I pushed past him to the outer door. "What do you care?"

He stepped out into the street, which was more alive now, with early workers and a soft, fresh breeze. He put his hands on his hips and glanced around, looking pleased with himself.

Then he registered that I was setting off townward. "Hey, where are you off to?"

"Work."

"Huh?" He was coming after me.

"You go home. Make Purl's day. It's weigh-day—she'll have time to spoil you."

He grabbed my arm. "Weigh-day already?"

"Yes. Let *go* of me!"

But he wanted an audience for his face, all gleeful and gratified. "Can I *believe* it? Can I believe my *luck*? Just in time for all the fun!"

I pulled free and hurried on—and he kept after me!, laughing all the way.

"Will you go *home*, please, Chirrup?"

"There's someone else I have to see first. Something I want to be in on."

I stopped in my tracks. Chirrup went on a few steps, then turned back to me. "And what do you mean, work? Shouldn't you be in school? Or must you puff up someone's pet at the last moment? What kind of Leet-licking have you graduated to, little sister?"

I was eyeing the hard-packed street-earth in front of me, but I knew exactly what merry expression he was wearing. I scratched the side of my face. "Are you going to go and see Purl, Chirrup?" I said softly.

He laughed. "I'm a free man, now, aren't I? I'll go and see who I like."

I made sure my fist came out of the blue, backhanding his handsome head, hard. It worked better than I could have imagined, sending him sprawling. And the look on his face, the shock (and some fear!)—I have to tell you, it warmed my bitter heart.

"Why, it was my *pleasure* to free you, Chirrup," I said. "No, no, don't thank me! The joy of having you back at the heart of our family will be *quite* sufficient."

And I walked on. My hand felt like a bag of burning bone-shards, but even if I never set another hair in place, it was worth it.

I went down to the beach, to one of the bathing huts, and changed into the weigh-clothes, and put on the make-up to cover my freckles. I unwound the false earlocks from the spoon handles I'd stored them on and taped them to my temples under the snood. Humming to myself, I stowed my Ord clothes under the floorboards of the hut, and set out for the weighing-hall.

The quickest way would have been through the Vines, but a snooded Leet wouldn't go there, so I went around by the avenues, trying not to hurry. Several people looked askance at me; I should have known I would look odd, moving on foot and alone.

It was better when I reached the basement lane behind the weighing-hall. Several Leet families were there, doing the distance from their equipages on foot to avoid the crowd out front, and Ords were also going about their basement business with cloth and gift and message-box.

Rustle's man was there, dressed as a florist's assistant. I strayed past him slowly, but his gaze glided over me and onward. The bouquet was a proper Leet one, crafted of acanthus and frail-hellebore, the stalks wrapped bulkily in fringed satin and ornamental paper.

"It's me," I muttered. "I am Rill." I held out my hands for the flowers.

He drew them away in startlement. "I was expecting someone more Ordinary," he said almost accusingly.

"Don't muck about. Just give me the stuff. Hell's fury, what's among these stalks—lead?"

"Sh! Just put it in the flower-wall with the others. Don't let a flower-man do it, he'll notice the weight. And try not to show it, the way you carry it. And here." He handed me a satin-wrapped box, also heavy, bound with glittering gift-cords. "See if you can't place this well up against the girls' corral. And then get out of there."

"Get *out*? But I thought I was there for the whole ceremony."

He blinked. He drew me aside as an emptied car went by, the way an Ord would draw aside a Leet.

"What, will it start leaking then and there?" I said.

"Leaking?"

"Leaking the smoke, or the smell, or whatever nuisance it is."

He looked up from securing my hands around the gift and flowers. Even for an Ord, he looked white. Even his lips were white, where they weren't freckled.

"What is it?" I said.

He lived again, a pale and trembling version of his former self. "Yes, it will start . . . leaking. But you do whatever Rus—whatever you've been told you should do. It's not for me to go against his orders—"

And he hurried from me. A family with a plain-snooded nubile man passed, and bowed to me, and I returned the bows, my face brushed by the petals of my lovely leaden flowers.

| | | |

Of course it was easy; everything is made easy for Leets. They are ushered here and there, welcomed everywhere; the door-guard did not even look at me, my garb and bearing were so convincing. I gave in my Key among the twittering nubiles and the graver voices of their parents. I passed from the key-arch into the gentle roar of the vast weighing-hall. I tried not to gawp like the awe-struck Ord I was.

Musicians were already playing in the upper galleries, casting a web of gentle, echoing prettiness out over the sea of other sounds. The whole place was all plastered and gilded and encrusted with Leet embellishment, but they had been unable to disguise the good bones of the Ord temple it had once been. The central circle of the sun-pattern on the floor, in olden times a plain gold-foil disc, was crowded with equipment for the ceremony— two low-backed chairs, two mirror-silver scales-dishes behind them, silver trays of snowy white cards and ink-brushes to be used in influencing the marriage-matches.

I descended the stairs from the entrance-gallery. I followed another lone woman who was carrying a bouquet, past the girls' corral, which was filling with white-gowned, bright-eyed, dazzling-haired nubiles. A curved metal flower-wall had been built around the central stone column in the far wall, of criss-crossed metal into which the stems of bouquets could be inserted.

"Shall I place that for you?" an attendant offered the woman in front of me.

"Thank you, I would prefer to do it myself. It is for my nephew."

"And yours, miss?"

"No, I will place mine, too, thank you," I said in a faultless accent.

"As you please. May I hold your gift while you place it?"

"Why, thank you. But take care with it; it is *verr-eh* fragile."

"I will," he assured me.

There was a space in the wall among several bouquets of pale orange lilies, at head-height. There I attempted to push the stalk-end of my bouquet. The grid opening seemed a little small—what would I do if it didn't fit? I heard the wrapping tear, and nervously pulled the bouquet halfway out again—and pushed it straight back in, hearing the wrapper give further, sure the whole room had seen those glints of force-metal among the stalks, those braided wires.

"It looks beautiful," said the attendant when I returned to him. With a thudding heart I smiled, relieved him of my gift, and moved by.

"Where would you like to be placed, miss?" said another.

"As near the young ladies as possible."

"May I take your gift and have it guarded during the ceremony?"

"Thank you, but I am quite comfortable carrying it. It is fragile, you see, and for a very special person."

"As you please, miss."

I was passed up an aisle and ushered to a cushioned bench seat right up against the girls' corral. I glanced across the hall at the boys, and among all the piled, coiled, fanciful hairstyles there—all of which would be unpinned in the course of the ceremony, tumbled down to nothing but their weight in the scales—I sought out the highest gleam there, the gold of golds, and yes!, it was Lar's. He was a-shimmer with nerves. It suited him.

I tucked the gift under my seat, up against the wooden wall of the corral. The crowd noise was growing, and the seats around me were filling. Superseding the smells of cold stone and bench-wax were the scents of hair-wash and cloth-freshener, and the cedar that was used in tamsin bedding to absorb their natural rank smell. I sat there breathing it all in. I had done it, the "big job" Chirrup had failed to do—not so big after all, eh? And because of my skills, I'd done it better than he ever could have; I'd brought the two nuisances right into the heart of Leet territory, right into the—

The gift moved, behind my slippered heel. "Look, mam," said a little voice behind me.

I turned and saw the gift rising, in hands too small for its weight. Slipping, slipping—the woven cane of the bench-back kept me from it. I gave a muted cry.

"Oh, Lossie, mustn't touch!" Lossie's mother caught the present as it slipped from his hands. "Oh, it's heavy!" she muttered, and through the cane I watched it stagger across the air with her hand chasing it below until *bang!*, it hit the side of the corral, with the mother's hand bracing it.

"Oh, *please* be careful!" I whispered.

"You should cloak such a thing," she said, handing it to me. "There are always lots of curious children here."

"I thank you." Warily I watched the parcel for the wisps of smoke that would betray me.

Another person had been squeezed onto my bench, and there was no longer any room for the gift beside me. I held it in my lap. The air was now very warm, and the girl next to me had a heavily perfumed tamsin—crudely augmented, too—and I felt slightly ill. I wondered if I was as white, behind my face-paint, as Rustle's man had been. *Get out of there*, he'd said. As if I'd miss this. As if I'd ever get another chance to watch a weighing ceremony, one of the highlights of the Leet calendar, *the* highlight of Lar's whole life!

And then my memory proffered me two pictures. A younger Chirrup at the kitchen table, tying up smell-bags to let off at school, cloths, powders, and fuses laid out neater than ever he laid out his study tools. Powders were how you made smells, not force-metal. And—I lifted the box in my lap doubtfully—powders weren't this heavy.

The other picture was more confused. Legs, soldiers, Purl pulling me away. I crane back; I see a soldier setting a time-piece into a patch of shining metal-paste at the base of a pillar. *But why?* I say. *Because it was a rebel meeting-house,* she answers. And she adds, when we're away from the crowd, *Because it was a thing of beauty, of Ord beauty, one of the few left.*

That was what you used force-metal for.

Surely not.

I rose and shakily placed the gift on my seat. "Excuse me," I said to the woman next to me. Her tamsin stretched out languidly to sniff at the gift-cord where my fingers had sweated on it. The girl tutted and minimally moved her knees, and all along the bench people began gathering in skirt and tamsin-paw and saying, "Oh really—You would think—Must you?"

I forced my way along them, apologising in my false voice, cursing them in my head. I trod on the toe of one lady's slipper and she hissed to her companion, "Manners of an Ordinary!" I was so *glad* to be an Ord, glad I didn't have to wear this daft cumbersome costume, glad I didn't have to closet myself with these pinheaded decorated people all the days of my life!

I stumbled out at the end of the bench, straightened my snood full of padding, hurried past all the attendants offering, "May I help—Is there something—?"

"All I need is air." And to get out, out!, before whatever was going to happen, happened. I had to force myself not to rudely push through the families and dignitaries flowing down the staircase.

I stood gasping in the sudden cool emptiness of the key-arch.

"Miss? For your return?" The attendant held up a Key, its slim chain swinging and shining. I took it, calm now, as good as away now. "Don't be long, or you'll miss the start of the ceremony."

I smiled. "I only need a moment or two." Folding Key and chain into my hand, I stepped outside.

It was quieter now, the equipages clearing from under the portico, the broad avenue beyond almost empty, for no normal Leet business or politicking went on on weigh-day. It was cool and clear, sunny and peaceful as I walked seaward, smiling at my panic of a few moments ago. All those unfamiliar smells must have affected me, the proximity to all those Leets, the strain of pretending to be Leet myself. Since when had rebel activities been truly dangerous? No one was ever *hurt*, either rebel or Leet.

There was no one on the beach, only sandpipers picking at the low-tide line, only wavelets turning over, glossy with the morning sun. I found the hut I'd used earlier, took off the heavy snood and gave my scalp a luxurious scratch. As I undressed I wondered, had Chirrup met with Rustle yet? Would Rustle say anything about me, about any of this? I wished I could be a fly on the wall for that meeting, wished I could see Chirrup's face. I wished I could have seen Lar's face, Lar's mother's, everyone else's, as they unloaded all that beautiful hair into the scales. I should've kept my head; what did I know about rebel methods? Maybe there was some new kind of smoke or smell you could make using force-metal. There must be, since rebels never caused anything worse than a nuisance—

First came the stunning noise of the bomb, then the shock. The wooden walls juddered and cracked, and I flung out my hands as if I could steady them. "No," I said very firmly. I scrabbled my own clothes on, over the Leet underwear, and ran out, up onto the promenade wall where I could see the city centre.

The verdigris dome of the weighing-hall lay tipped in the cup of the walls, rakish as a scholar's cap. The second blast—from the bouquet against the pillar—blew out all the walls. They hung a moment as stone lace, then sank, as the dome sank, into a vast soft uprising of dirty smoke.

"No. No. It's not possible."

Get out of there, Rustle's florist-man had said.

"They don't do this kind of thing!"

And then he'd whitened. *Whatever you've been told to do,* he'd said.

"No-no-no-no-*no*!"

It's not for me to go against his orders.

"Oh, no." I clutched my stomach as if someone had just punched me. "Not for you to step in and *save my life* or anything. *Dastard* Rustle! Can't kill off my brother so *I'll do,* will I?"

Then the Trades Hall blew, just across the Vines. The explosion thumped me sideways off the wall. Then something else, bigger, farther, went up. I scrambled back onto the wall and stood on my toes to see. The spires of the bourse buildings no longer adorned our skyline. With a roar the specialists' shops threw themselves into the Vines; with a thud, my college (my colleagues! my teachers!) made a puff of dust among the apartments to the west. The Protocol Prison—with Chirrup's empty cell in it—blew a great hole open in the Wall.

Someone behind me on the promenade, a terrified

minor Leet, began to scream, "Everything's going! Everything!" And a common voice cried joyfully, "Yes, everything—at last! The rebels! Our man Rustle! Praise heaven!"

And the bombs kept on.

I was running. There were lost and frantic Leets, half-dressed, all through the Vines; there were Ords, thick-freckled brick-dusters, swarming in the Avenue of the Conquerors, cheering, loosing their long hair from caps and kerchiefs. Stones were falling from the sky—I saw a street guard felled by a flying gargoyle off a Wall-turret—and all the air was hazy and unstable.

I was running home. Ours was an Ord sector; nothing would blow there. But I could not get past the weighing-hall bridge; all the lanes were blocked with fallen masonry.

A man was screaming out pain and terror from the rubble in front of me, Ord or Leet I could not see for smoke. His screams had a strange, open-air sound where they should have echoed from wall to wall.

I would have gone to him, but the smoke caught me by the throat and brought me to my knees, carrying with it from the flaming weigh-hall the sharp, rich, disgusting smell of burning hair.

| | | |